THE FARTHEST REACHES

CLINT WESTGARD

ALSO BY CLINT WESTGARD

Published by Lost Quarter Books
www.lostquarterbooks.com

This edition 2017

Cover design by James, GoOnWrite.com

ISBN: 978-1-928035-27-5

For Dad, for inspiring my love of science fiction.

CONTENTS

BEWARE!
THE SEAS ARE ANGRY THIS NIGHT

"Captain, I don't know what to tell you. The game has changed."

The dwarf peered sullenly through the haze filled cavern, rank with the smell of refuse, at the dandy who was smiling and smoking a thin cigarillo.

"Anger troubles the blood," the dandy said in a sympathetic voice, his smile deepening. The expression on the henchman who stood behind him, his hands hanging free at his sides, as though he were waiting an excuse to use them, did not change.

"Daftness," the dwarf said. He was dressed in sailor's clothes, as was his companion, a giant of a man with hands as large as the dwarf's head. They had docked that afternoon and made their way through the city and then below, through the sewers, to this room, as had been agreed. The sewers were ancient and huge, no longer in use, the sole memories of a long extinct civilization. They still retained the shadow of the grandeur that had once existed aboveground, long disappeared, replaced by haphazard and crumbling edifices.

"The Grand Jefe will not be happy. He's no faro man."

"He will play," the dandy said. "It's all been arranged. There's no need to trouble yourself with his concerns."

"I will decide what to trouble myself with."

The dandy shrugged.

"Daftness," the dwarf said and spat on the ground. "What have you done?"

"As I said, it has all been arranged. A new sun rises tomorrow," the dandy said, spreading his hands. He looked at the henchman as if he might confirm that indeed it was so.

"Arranged? What daftness is this? What's been arranged? What have you done?" Spittle flew from the dwarf's mouth as he said it.

"It hardly matters to you, but I am keeping the Infernal Contraption. It is no longer for sale."

"It has already been promised to someone. We set sail tonight."

"The seas are angry this night, captain."

"All nights."

The dandy made a show of looking at his shoes, though he still kept his eyes on the two of them. He threw the stub of his cigarillo away and stepped toward the dwarf, holding both hands before him.

"I don't know what else to tell you. It is not for sale."

"The thing is not yours. It is for the Grand Jefe to decide," the dwarf growled. "Now let's stop with this nonsense. The hour's getting late."

Here the dandy's smile grew. "As to that, there are great many things that are no longer for the Grand Jefe to decide."

"We'll see what he has to say when I tell him that you've squared the deal."

"You'll not be seeing him anytime soon."

As the dandy spoke the henchman stepped from behind him holding an antiquated handpiece. Before anyone had a chance to move further the giant leapt towards the henchman, moving with a surprising quickness, and got hold of his wrist and neck in his massive hands. The sound of grinding bone was followed by an airless scream from the henchman, more felt by the two who watched than heard. The gun fell from the henchman's hand and the echoes of its clattering had only just dimmed when he followed it to the ground. The dandy watched with disbelieving eyes.

"The game is changed," the dwarf said and was at the dandy's throat with a knife. There was a gurgling of blood as air, arteries and saliva mixed for a propulsive moment and then the dandy collapsed, writhing for a time before going still.

"Quick Rene," the dwarf said, wiping his hands and blade clean, "We need to find the Infernal Contraption and be on our way."

They began a search of the adjoining chambers, all dark and overgrown with mold. Within one the dwarf found stacks of wooden crates, which he called for the giant to open. Inside they found stacks of arquebuses, along with balls and powder. The dwarf hissed at the site of them, "Daftness. The fool was planning a war."

A new thought gave the dwarf pause and his eyes widened and his face went pale. "The game is changed," he whispered to himself.

"I thought it was faro."

"Quiet Rene."

"It's a fine enough game if the dealer is straight," the giant continued.

"The whole world's gone queer," the dwarf said.

"Well, if those are the rules, then we play by them."

"Daftness. Anarcho-syndicalist," the dwarf spat at the giant and headed into the next chamber.

It was empty, but beyond it was a hallway shrouded in gloom, the scent of burnt kerosene and some other ineffable darkness on the air. He shuddered at the smell and started into the hallway, motioning for the giant to hold a lantern high to guide their way. At the end of the hallway they stepped into a small room, so low-ceilinged the giant had to crouch to fit within. The lantern illuminated the Infernal Contraption, which filled nearly the entire chamber. It was a fantastical arrangement of tubes and kettles, reservoirs of glass and iron and crystal, spheres linked to cubes by twisting and warped cylinders. A tremendous heat emanated from somewhere within, produced by the combustion of some extraordinary mineral. It powered the engine, which moved silently, but for a regular shuddering of gears that was followed by a puff of vapor, a suffocating damp.

The dwarf gasped hearing this and feeling the kiss of the contraption's calumniating breath. He leapt from the room, going at a run back down the hallway not even waiting for the giant and the lantern. "Blast," he said, "He's turned the thing on. Madness."

When he had returned to the main chamber where the dandy and the henchman still lay he stopped to gather himself, closing his eyes and trembling violently, the thought of the contraption and its malformed air overwhelming him. To die by the hand of vapors, of the very air that he breathed. He wiped at his face as though the pestilence had coated it. The giant emerged from the warren of chambers looking at the dwarf with a quizzical expression.

"We must be quits Rene."

"What are those, captain?"

"Immaterial. We must go then. Quickly. There will be a new sun tomorrow, a new city entire. The Grand Jefe will not be pleased when he learns what's gone on here, and he won't be picky in choosing who to blame."

As he turned to flee the sewers, the dandy's corpse caught his eye and he crouched over it. "What were you thinking? You'd have likely destroyed yourself as lived to see the morrow. Fool."

There was a ring on one the dandy's finger, gold with a blood red stone set within. The dwarf grunted and pulled it off, placing it on his own thumb, where it rested easily. He stood up and admired it and then motioned to the giant, who seized both bodies and dragged them back to the sewers. As he let them slip into the putrid river that still flowed by, he wondered aloud whether if a thing was without matter it could still be a thing.

"Quiet Rene. And be quick about it," the dwarf said. "If what the man said is true..."

"The game is changed?"

"Unequivocally."

They retraced their steps through the sewer's warren of tunnels, the dwarf scuttling ahead and the giant following in his wake holding the lantern high above the other's head. They appeared oblivious to the stench, moving deftly along the broken walkways that connected the tunnels. The dwarf muttered to himself the whole while, stopping here and there to scout different byways, at one point even pulling a piece of paper from his pocket and turning it round and round as he studied it under the lamplight. At last, after much wandering and doubling back, all with hurried glances over his shoulder at the slightest noise, the dwarf found what he sought, a grand staircase that led above to the city.

They emerged to a metropolis glorious with sound and color, a pageantry submerged in the gloom of the day's end, enervated by the sparking lamps illuminating each corner. The streets were thronged with people, harmony and chaos arm in arm, speaking a hundred tongues. Their shadows danced above them, as dragons and warlocks in mortal combat. Across from where they stood a band had set up and was playing to the passersby, an outfit with a harp, banjo and bone saw. Many onlookers had begun to dance, making their passage nearly impossible.

The dwarf was beside himself. "It is the world's end here."

"How so?"

"Can't you see Rene?" The giant shrugged and scratched behind his ear.

The dwarf shuddered, as though warding off some awful premonition, and led the giant in the opposite direction

The city had changed since they had journeyed through its streets earlier. It had been a festival evening, the whole town seemingly moving about the avenues in a feverish celebration. They had found themselves surrounded at various points in their journey by swords swallowers, flame spitters, jugglers and caperers, along with various and sundry others, all in colorful dress and masks. Now it had transformed into something uglier, the revelry of the chaotic throngs mutated so that now it was filled with menace and fear. The cries that filled the air around them sounded like shouts of terror and anguish. There were men with swords on every corner, their heads covered, speaking to each other in hushed tones as they watched the proceedings.

Considering these ominous portents and what they might foretell, the dwarf sought to forgo the streets where it seemed they were more likely to encounter trouble , at least until they found themselves out of the city center. The alleys were little better though, the first one they tried to go down had several men getting beaten by the masked sword-bearers, while in another they watched as several men pinned a struggling girl to the ground. The dwarf, muttering to himself, led them away before they saw any more.

"Keep your wits about you," he told the giant, sticking his own hand inside his jacket so that he could finger the pommel of his dagger.

"Where?" the giant asked, stopping in the street to pat his pockets.

"Daftness. Irrevocable and complete," the dwarf said and gave the giant a kick in the shin.

They dodged their way around a few streets where

brawls had broken out, the air thick with smoke from a building someone had set alight. The wind shifted as they walked and a hint of the infectious fumes the dandy had unleashed below them reached their nostrils. The dwarf recoiled at it, cursing, and he leapt off the street into the nearest building, as though that might somehow quarantine them from the pestilence. He found himself in the empty waiting room of a brothel, at the foot of a long and curving staircase that led to a balcony and beyond.

One of the harlots emerged from above, roused by the giant's noisy entrance, a young thing with heavy shadows under her eyes. "Nothing's on offer tonight boys," she said to them wearily.

"No one in this blasted town seems to understand the basic principles of commodification," the dwarf said.

"Maybe it's the person doing the buying."

"My coin will stand the same as anyone's."

The girl smiled. "Too bad the rest of you don't have the girth of your eyes."

"Daftness," the dwarf said. "We have to time for this. The city is in its last breath."

The girl frowned and took a step down the stair towards them. "That's a queer thing to say. What do you mean?"

"You smell it on the air as well as I. The world is shadows now."

"Yes," she said, "Yes, I do. What is it?"

The dwarf smiled. "It is the unmaking of this city. A very stupid fool has started the Infernal Contraption in the sewers below us. When it is through all that will remain are the echoes of things."

"Why would anyone build such a thing?"

"Daftness. If it can be built, it will be."

The girl seemed perplexed. "But if all it can do is unmake things, and it cannot be controlled, then how could anyone dare use it?"

"Oh, someone will always believe that they can control

it. Perhaps someone can, I am no engineer."

"It is just madness."

The dwarf waved at her. "Well, every dance ends and we must be certain we are still substantial when it does.

"I thought we were quits?" Rene said.

"Daftness. Yes. We still have time. Lead the way."

They left the harlot to her empty parlor and plunged again into the overwhelming streets, the dwarf checking periodically over his shoulder to see if anyone was following in their wake. The crowds thinned as they went, though the masked men with the swords were still on every other street. They were careful to avoid them, for the signs of their brutality were present on the faces of many they passed. At last, and with relief, they came to an empty street, strewn with refuse and littered with puddles of stagnant water, though it had not rained that day. Only one lamp was lit, and that on the corner at the far end of the street. Even in the dim light afforded them here they could see the black grime that infested the cracked walls of the buildings on either side of them.

As they moved forward a man stepped out of the shadows, his face and hands obscured, so that he appeared to be a ghoul. Behind them another appeared, cutting off their escape, his hand in his jacket clutching a dagger or handpiece.

"Bugger all," the dwarf said with a shake of his head.

The man in before them stepped out of the gloom, revealing the angular details of his face and grinned at them. "Give me your dreams," he said, tipping back the crown that stood perilously askew on his head.

The dwarf looked up at him grimly, not answering.

"Come now," the man said jauntily. "Do you not recognize who rules these parts? Hand them over promptly."

"Daftness," the dwarf muttered under his breath. "Absolute and unequivocal."

The giant glanced back and forth, from one face to

the other, nervously.

"I have spoken. Commanded even. If my jurisdiction is defied there must be consequences. There will be repercussions."

"Poppycock," the man positioned behind them said.

"If blood must be spilt then blood will be spilt of course," the man said, looking them over sympathetically. "I know it's rather draconian, but these are times we live in after all."

"Poppycock," the other fellow said, stepping from behind them to give his companion a shove for good measure. "You are mad. Do not listen to him I tell you. He has no authority here. Where are his guards? His servants? His courtiers and court? They do not exist."

"As to that," the first man confided to them, "I am a beggar you see. It makes enforcement of my decrees rather difficult I grant. But my crown is undeniable, you must admit."

"Admit nothing."

The king patted the other consolingly on his arm. "My queen," he said with a patient smile.

"Some drunken lout handed it over to him earlier this evening," the queen said, ignoring him, "Before passing out in an alley. He won it gambling from some lush of a nobleman."

"It is not the most storied lineage, I will allow. But, as I am a benevolent ruler for the most part, I will let this overlarge fellow here settle the debate. What do I look like?" he asked, tipping his crown forward.

The giant stared at the King baffled, but the dwarf kicked him in the shins and so he spoke: "Well. You are in rags mostly. Filthy ones. And your stench is foul. Your hair is as wild as your eyes and you have no shoes, but you are wearing a crown, though it seems a bit battered."

"It was made from pennies," the Beggar King said proudly. "So, you see, I am clearly exactly what I say I am. And now I really must insist, before this continues any further, that you hand over your dreams. I am rather short on them at the moment. No offense meant," he added, with a nod to the dwarf.

"Anarcho-syndicalist," the dwarf could not contain himself.

"This is not real," the queen said, "You have simply dressed yourself up like this. You have no kingdom. You have no ambassadors or knights. And you cannot take dreams. No manner of being can do this. It is impossible, it is absolutely ridiculous."

"My queen, my queen," the Beggar King said, as though talking to a child, "You see, you have already given me yours."

"Give them back," the queen said, clutching at the lapels of the man's ruined coat while the other consoled him. The dwarf motioned hurriedly behind his back, and both he and the giant made a quick retreat back the way they had come. The last they heard was the King admonishing the other sternly. "Well, first you must petition me. There are protocols to follow after all."

Their fortunes took a turn for the better following this incident. After making their way back around, skirting the King's domain, they came into a large square decorated by a few broken statues. The dwarf scampered up the nearest and from its pinnacle he could make out the sails of the ships at dock hanging in the air above the teetering buildings, looking as though they too might wash away with the tide. The dwarf clapped his hands in delight, "Not a moment too soon."

They started down the street that appeared to lead to the shore, but soon found themselves trapped in a warren of pathways leading in all directions, stairways ascending and descending abruptly in their midst.

"Daftness," the dwarf said, eyeing the maze before picking a stairway at random and plunging up the steps.

They emerged to smoke and ruins. Before them was a cemetery without markers, the wrecked bones of the dead strewn about haphazardly, the fresh earth from their disinterment the only proof that they had once been buried. There seemed to be no source for the smoke, unless the atmosphere itself was alight. Or, perhaps it was just that here all the infectious fumes of the Infernal Contraption had gathered and turned venomous. The dwarf cast about nervously but there seemed no way around the graveyard without a retreat, which he dared not chance with the labyrinth behind them and their sails within sight.

"Mind yourself Rene, these are dangerous parts," the dwarf said and strode forward to meet the gloom. The giant followed, wondering aloud as to which of his parts were dangerous, but the dwarf ignored him, his eyes cast ahead and his hand on his dagger.

At the cemetery's center, in the midst of what remained of the shattered crypts that had once held the deceased from the wealthiest families of the city, they came upon a pit filled with smoldering ashes of what smelled like flesh and tar. They crept by this, the dwarf shaking his head in horror, fearful of somehow being drawn into the conflagration, but hoping the smoke was thick enough it would cover their passage.

They were nearly past it when they found themselves confronted by a man in the finery of some obscure religious order. In his hand was a rake, which he had been using to stir the dark and viscous byproduct of the fires as it bubbled over the shallow confines of the pit, flowing back towards the center of the city. The dwarf stopped, keeping his distance and motioning for the giant to do the same, while he waited to see what the man would do.

He nodded towards the pit and said, "They were their own executioners."

The dwarf swallowed, his eyes watering from the smoke. "Just so," he said.

"A worthy end." The man smiled and then, spying the ring on the dwarf's hand, said, "Such a fine jewel."

"This," the dwarf said. "A mere bauble. A trinket. Hardly worth the effort of putting it on. It's a family keepsake."

"Is a man's life, even one spanned as short as yours, worth a trifle?"

The dwarf grimaced and pulled out his dagger, motioning to the giant to ready himself.

"You think that has any power here in this realm," the man said, pressing his hands together as though to pray. "Can not a vapor kill a man as easily as a blade?"

The dwarf laughed bitterly. "You think you can ride that dragon now that it is unleashed? Many have tried and the tempest has torn them apart."

"We shall see," the man said and closed his eyes, murmuring an invocation to himself. The dwarf studied him, waiting to see if this were some manner of feint or sleight of hand, but the man stayed as he was, lost in his contemplation.

He was just turning to tell the giant that they should go while they had the chance when Rene said, "Well that is unusual."

The giant was pointing at the pit where the ashen tar was bubbling forth. The liquid began to cohere into shapes and for a moment it appeared as though it were filled with drowning men, all an instant from being absorbed forever. But then, one by one, they extracted themselves from the boiling mass taking tentative steps upon the ground.

"Madness. Unequivocal," the dwarf and then looked at the giant, "Run you fool, while we still have time."

They took off across the cemetery grounds, leaping over the noxious stream spilling out of the pit, which, once they were past, quickly formulated itself into more pursuers. The cleric laughed madly at them as they went, calling on his minions to seize the dwarf and his ring. The dwarf stumbled and scrambled over the refuse left from the desecrated tombs, while the giant loped along beside him, picking him up by the shoulder when their pursuers got too close. The walls that marked the graveyards boundary were soon in sight and the dwarf had just turned to tell the giant that he must take them both over, when a dozen of the creatures emerged from the nearby graves and blocked their path.

They were soon joined by the other pursuers and all of the creatures pressed in close around the two, leering at them with their malevolent eyeless faces, their mouths open in a gaping wordless snarl. The dwarf shrank to his knees, raising his hands to ward off the creatures, while the giant took a violent swing at the nearest. His blow did not land, passing right through the thing, leaving only viscous traces of the tar and being on his hand. The giant studied his hand, opening and closing it, confused by what had happened, but the dwarf, seeing it, sprang to his feet in delight and plunged his hand carrying the ring into the nearest of the monsters.

The creatures halted, confused and hesitating, cocking their heads from the dwarf to where the ring had disappeared in the inky mass. The dwarf held it there, ignoring the chilling cold of the vaporous being's insides, so strange given the creatures' provenance in that hellish pit. Their awkward standoff continued until the cleric broke his minions' reverie with a cry to seize the ring no matter the cost.

Sensing the moment, the dwarf pulled his hand free and held it up with a flourish, the ring gone. The creatures all studied him, as though suspecting some kind of trickery, but when none was apparent they turned from him and fell upon their comrade, tearing at his dripping limbs. Not waiting for them to finish their work, the dwarf and giant fled the gruesome scene, passing through the creatures where they stood. They did not halt until they were over the wall and out of breath, well beyond the graveyard's border.

They waited on the narrow side street they found themselves on, both of them trying to wring out the noxious fluid that was staining their clothes, while the dwarf watched to see that no pursuers had followed them. When he was satisfied that they had made good on their escape he set off in the direction of the docks, cursing under his breath at the overwhelming stench that now permeated his clothes and skin, the giant trailing in his wake. After they had gone a few more blocks the dwarf reached into his shirt pocket where he had secreted the ring and placed it back upon his thumb, admiring its glint in the dim glow of the street lanterns.

The rest of their journey passed without incident, the streets near the wharf almost empty of people. There was, to the dwarf's eye, fewer sails now visible on the dock, which suggested that some vessels had fled, hardly surprising given the events of the evening. The conflagration they had left was spreading behind them. There was smoke hanging over everything and even the glow of flames was visible in a few spots, though it only served to illuminate the spreading darkness. The scent of the malformed air was faint here, but it would arrive soon enough and they hurried along to be certain they would not be in port once it did.

By the time they arrived at the docks the moon had passed from the sky and the first hints of the sun's rising were illuminating the far horizon. As they made their way to their ship's berth one of the dock girls, a platypus faced woman, wandered over to them, a smile twisting her lips.

"Where are you headed sailors?" she asked them.

"Bugger off," the dwarf said, a giddy smile painting his lips, the ship now in sight.

"Suit yourself," the girl said. "You drift from port to port and to what gain I ask you? Those places are no different than here."

"Not after tonight," the dwarf said. "Not after tonight. We shall not return after tonight."

"And if the seas are angry?"

The voice came from behind them and sounded as

though the speaker had drawn on a pipe as he spoke. The dwarf swore under his breath and turned to face this new arrival. He found himself facing a finely appointed palanquin carried by slaves. Two men with swords stood beside it and one pulled aside the palanquin's curtain to reveal a man dressed in a marvelously colored kaftan, diamonds on his fingers and at his throat. The dwarf bowed.

"Grand Jefe. It's a mean existence, no doubt. But it is existence, of that I can be assured."

"Are you so sure?"

The dwarf bowed again. "Nothing stands solid on the seas."

"True," the Grand Jefe said in his wheezing voice. "And the land can shake and crumble as well. I fear tonight may be such a time. Our mutual acquaintance, young Dandy Slim, has failed to come to my villa to inform me of the success of our shared venture. No one has seen him about tonight, which is very strange given he is a nocturnal creature."

The dwarf eyed the Grand Jefe for a moment, seeming to judge the distance between himself and the potentate's two henchmen and then to his ship beyond. "We had much the same concern. He was nowhere to be seen, and not a whisper of what we were to receive from him was to be heard."

"Strange that you should say that," the Grand Jefe said. "Having been forced from my abode to attend to this most vexing issue, I cannot help but notice something even more problematic. The wind carries the whisper of what you were to receive on it. Your nose is not so short it is bereft of all sense I assume."

The dwarf nodded, unwilling to say anything just yet.

"And now I find you," the Grand Jefe continued, "Fleeing the city as it burns around you, empty handed. And I am left to wonder just what has occurred."

"As I said, we saw not a whisper of him. He was not at

the rendezvous."

"I must ask, then, how his ring came to be upon your finger." The two henchmen unsheathed their swords and arrayed themselves on either side of the palanquin at a motion from the Grand Jefe. The dwarf's expression did not change.

The dwarf spat on the docks. "I have not failed in my contractual obligations. My coffers will be as empty as yours this night. That fool dandy refused to give us the engine. He'd already turned it on. Said he was planning on taking the city from you."

"A useful story, no doubt," the Grand Jefe said. "But no one will take this city from me. Dandy Slim knew that well, though it seems you require a lesson."

"A new sun rises tomorrow regardless. The Infernal Contraption promises that."

"That may be, but I still hold the keys to all the doors."

"Of that I have no doubt," the dwarf said, bowing again. "Certainly you hold the keys to all the doors we require here, which is why I would be loathe to stand against you. But if we must stand apart after tonight, then I will do what must be done."

"You will loose this beast upon us I suppose." The Grand Jefe pointed at the giant. The dwarf said nothing, his eyes never leaving the Grand Jefe's.

"Very well," he said at last. "Know this though. Only the seas shall have you. Every port will be a figment for you. The only kindness granted you will be from the depths when you go to that cold embrace. So enjoy your existence, for it is all that is left you. Look one last time at what you are abandoning before you speak."

The dwarf turned and looked over the city as instructed and an expression of fierce longing appeared and then was quashed from his features. Without looking back he said, "If it is to be exile, then so be it."

"It is not exile, it is oblivion," the Grand Jefe said with a terrible finality and raised his hand. The two henchmen sheathed their swords and moved back alongside the palanquin, one of them pulling the curtain closed.

"Daftness," the dwarf muttered as he and the giant walked on to their ship. "We will be the substance of the thing."

"That was somewhat odd," the giant said.

"Quiet Rene. If we stay any longer we'll rot and go mad."

With that he broke into a trot, the giant a step behind. They hit the gangplank running.

THE PURPOSE OF THE SYSTEM

DISPATCH ONE

The air hisses, like a sigh expiring, as the airlocks link. Hidden gears turn, interlocking, the vessel and the habitat system speaking to each other, and at last the alarm sounds, notifying us that the doors are opening. The alarm continues to pulse, the light above the joined airlocks blinking red in unison with it. I adjust my metabolism, speeding it up from slow time, trying to time it so I reach my normal rates as the door opens and I have to move forward. I need to conserve my energy. There is no telling when I will be able to replenish myself.

Objective: CNS. Habitat A1.

A map of the habitat materializes in my mind as the thought is given voice. I see our path through the habitat to where the CNS is situated. Our target. The going will be easy until the first junction with the outer ring. After that, we will need some luck. Luck, the System's Trojans and malware, and the System itself to guide us.

Only six of us exit the vessel, not the planned twenty-five. Those left behind did not emerge from the depths of stasis when the System alerted us to our imminent arrival. No information had been offered as to their status and I did not bother to query. They are no longer relevant to the objective.

I can hear the others whisper their invocations to the System, as we pass through the air lock, and I join them. "System guide us. System protect us. We will heed your call."

The air in the habitat smells sweet, with hints of the sea, vegetation and earth, none of which exist here. The scent has been manufactured, I assume, for those that maintain the habitat. It seems an outrageous luxury in a place where strict functionality is the rule. The habitat's purpose is to house the CNS, which runs the entire fleet. The Intelligence. There should be nothing extraneous, and yet the smell said otherwise.

We had infected the habitat. The System had, at least. Or other agents in its service. It was not important; we were all the System, all cells in its larger body, subjugated to the larger cause. We had infected this Intelligence, allowing our vessel to dock with the habitat and allowing us entry without being incinerated by the various firewalls. Now we had to evade its secondary security protocols, no mean feat for the six of us remaining.

I feel no fear, in fact, I feel nothing. My emotional dampeners are functioning. Logically, I know, we are all very likely to die. Our individual odds of survival are miniscule, our chances of success only slightly greater. But I am ready. We are all ready for what is to come.

DISPATCH TWO

I dreamed, I was certain of it, though such a thing was not possible in stasis. The images were fleeting, flickers in my data stream, enough so that I could almost tell myself they were messages from the System. But they were not. They were my own thoughts.

The unending streams of data—the intel and subvocalizations of my fellow chosen, my internal health sensors, and above all the System's voice, with its constant intel updates and objectives—lulled me in my stasis, a comfort. That was what made the dream so disconcerting. It interrupted the streams, drowned them out, leaving me, in a sense, alone with my thoughts. It was utterly terrifying, or would have been, if I had not been in stasis, with my emotional dampeners active.

I saw myself standing before the Intelligence, blood pooling at my feet. I felt a touch of pain that was rapidly dimmed, my body responding with adrenaline and other dampeners. There was a taste of tin in my mouth. Blood as well, I realized. In my hands was my still-beating heart. I held it up to the Intelligence as though in offering.

DISPATCH THREE

"Do we know what happened to the rest of them?"
"No."
Neary did not look at me or subvocalize anything, but I can sense the eyebrow raised in question at my response. His feelings echo my own. How had the majority of a humanoid squad been neutralized without an apparent attack on the vessel? I had been in stasis, Neary in slow time maintaining the vessel and the rest of us, and neither of us knew. The data stream around those events, when I query it, is blank, which is most troubling of all.

The System is untroubled by this absence, informing us both that there was no loss of data during the voyage.

The blank in the stream is a type 2 standard error. Occurrence is less than 0.01% during normal function. Normal function conditions existed during the time parameter indicated. Testing indicates a standard error. No further action necessary.

"All clear ahead." Goodman announces.

Proceed to Entry Point Beta at double time. Confirm status.

Neary and I go forward as instructed, weapons charged and ready, alert to any movement, any change in the data streams. None occurs. The outer ring of the habitat, by all appearances, is not populated.

The Intelligence continues to, either, be unaware of our presence or, more likely, not to perceive us as intruders. Our infection is spreading, System be praised.

And if the place is uninhabited, as it seems, we might be able to penetrate its various security protocols without issue. I doubt that myself. The infection will be noticed, defenses will be turned against it and then us.

Neary and I arrive at the Beta Entry Point to the inner ring. Neary attends to the entry point, a sealed door with ocular identity scans required, while I watch the hallway to our rear.

The smell of outdoors that had clung to outer habitat ring is attenuated here, the scent suggesting something damp and musty. More than that, it smells noxious, maybe even toxic. The data streams inform me that is not the case. The place is pristine. Environmental controls remain in full effect. The smell, though, suggests decay.

"Do you smell that?" I subvocalize to Neary.

"Negative," is the instant response. "Air is pure."

The System informs me of the particulates present in the air, as well as its constitution: 16.53% oxygen, 82.11% nitrogen, 0.63 % argon, 0.65 carbon dioxide, and 0.08% trace elements. Percentages unchanged in the last hour. I breathe in and out and in, and still the smell remains.

DISPATCH FOUR

Position report.

"Unchanged," both Neary and I subvocalize simultaneously.

There is a pause, of only a few microseconds, but noticeable to both of us, from the System. It is both eerie and utterly disconcerting. The System does not think, it is. It exists. It does not pause.

We have secured the Beta Entry Point to the inner rings of the habitat and now await further instruction. The inner ring, based on the data stream intel and my own observation is as uninhabited as the outer ring. Has the entire habitat been evacuated? And if so, why?

This is not at all what we expected. The System told us to prepare for full defenses, not an abandoned habitat. It is best not to speculate. The Intelligence is still fully functioning and it could take its own defensive measures, regardless of whether humanoids are present to maintain its operations.

Proceed immediately to Alpha Entry Point. Use triple time. No response from Alpha team. Investigate and report. Use all caution.

System protect us.

Neary steps from the corridor and I follow behind,

protecting our rear, both us moving at triple time.

DISPATCH FIVE

"Pwaja inactive," Neary subvocalizes. "No sign of Garris."

I scan our immediate surroundings, keeping watch as Neary investigates further. There is no sign of anyone, no sign of activity beyond standard parameters from the Intelligence.

"Alpha Entry Point clear. Inner ring corridor clear. Beginning second sweep."

I do not glance at Neary as he flips over Pwaja's prone body and connects himself to it. Someone or something attacked him, there seems no other explanation, and a hostile encounter must be assumed to be imminent.

"Pwaja deceased," Neary subvocalizes. "Proximate cause: weapon's discharge."

Not the Intelligence then, which is something of a relief. It is still unaware of our presence.

"Have you determined location of Garris?" I subvocalize.

Negative. No known location.

I freeze where I am in my surveillance circuit and I can feel Neary go still behind me.

"Do you have location of Gamma team?" Neary asks.

There is the barest hint of stress in his tone, which is concerning. With emotional dampeners in effect he needs to be extremely stressed for any sign to be visible.

Affirmative.

"Why are you unable to locate Garris?" I query.

There is another worrying pause, a fraction of a second, enough for me to descend into darkness momentarily.

Garris is no longer connected to the System.

"That is not possible," Neary says, aloud this time.

His voice, though barely more than a whisper startles me and I whirl to face him, weapon ready for discharge.

Confirmed.

DISPATCH SIX

Both Neary and I attempt to contact Garris. There is no response.

Objective revised. Continue in pursuit of Garris. Determine if active. Neutralize.

The Gamma team is to carry on and try to reach the CNS. How they are to do this without the support of either the Alpha or the Beta teams is not given voice to. None of us spoke of our own doubts, though I'm certain Neary and the others feel them just as I do.

But it does not matter. We must trust the System regardless. If we are to be sacrificed, as it appears we are, it cannot be without purpose. The System is the purpose in the end.

The System orders us forward, deeper into the inner ring of the habitat, though the data streams offer no evidence that Garris has gone in this direction, as opposed to retreating back to the outer ring. The greatest danger to us in many ways, assuming he has somehow betrayed us, lay in his seizing control of our vessel and thereby stranding us here.

That is irrelevant to the System, though. It is only concerned with ensuring our objective is successfully met.

Ensuring Garris did not interfere with that is, therefore, our objective. We are expendable.

So it shall be. These thoughts all flicker through my mind, intermingling with the data stream, taking only microseconds. Bitterness at my fate is felt and suppressed in the time it takes me to blink. Introspection is a luxury.

We move at normal time, conserving energy and exercising caution. I fully expect Garris to be dead somewhere. Has the Intelligence managed to override his System connections somehow, substituting its own data stream? The System has, as yet, been unable to latch on to its data streams, so we are operating in the blind in that regard.

There is something to the thought though. There are the blanks in the data stream, mysterious to say the least. The pauses in the System are unheard of, to my knowledge. The smell and my dream, both impossibilities according to the System.

Anomalies? Ghosts in the machines? Or something more sinister?

I do not hear the pulse as the weapon discharges. There is the briefest of flashes in the corner of my eye. Time enough for me to notice, but not to react.

DISPATCH SEVEN

Darkness.

More than darkness. A void. No data stream, no surveillance, no senses.

I reach out for the System but it is not there. I try to subvocalize, to call Neary or the Gamma team, but no sound emerges.

Silence.

DISPATCH EIGHT

Confirm. Objective Garris. Neutralize. Last known location contact Corridor 48. Confirm.

The darkness lifts, like mist evaporating in the sun, the air hazy with waves. I blink to clear my eyes, feeling lightheaded. My body attempts to compensate.

I can see myself again, standing before the System, arms outstretched in offering. My heart is in my hands and my chest has a gaping hole where I cut it from. There is a smile on my face.

Confirm. Rendezvous with Neary. Confirm. Objective Garris. Confirm. Proceed to Junction 7G. Confirm.

Waves of nausea assault me as my body compensates to the weapon's discharge. Everything aches. My dampeners are still functioning normally, which means I am severely injured. The data stream is present but makes no sense. The intel it provides is garbled, nonsense. Part of me knows it is not the data stream; I simply cannot interpret it at this moment.

System provide, System provide.

Confirm. Contact. Confirm. Respond.

I manage to get myself up and into a seated position, propping myself against the nearest wall. A quick self-assessment reveals no external injuries. My weapon is in my hands. I try to stand and the world becomes a point of light and then goes black. I slump back into the wall. My breathing sounds ragged, mucus filled. I cough loudly, the sound echoing down the corridor.

"Garris sighted. Confirmed. Corridor 57. Junction 3D. Okimba. Neary. Please respond."

I cough again and moan at the ache in my chest. I can feel the reconstruction response beginning, the nanocytes whirling into action, although I understand that is total delusion. I cannot feel to that level. The data stream can inform me, but I can only access it intermittently at the moment.

Confirm. Revised objective. Locate Neary. Neutralize. Confirm.

That is wrong, I know. Garris is to be neutralized, not Neary. Where was he? He was beside me when…The System speaks and we obey. We are the System and it is us.

"Garris engaged. Confirmed. Corridor 57. Junction 3D. Okimba. Neary. Please respond. Support required."

Confirm. Contact. Confirm. Respond. Revised objective. Confirm.

The System speaks and we obey. We are the System.

DISPATCH NINE

I find Neary at Junction 8E, bent over on his knees, clutching his head in agony. He does not look up as I approach, nor does he seem to notice as I complete a circuit around him, confirming that no one else is lurking down any of the corridors.

"Neary sighted," I subvocalize. "Confirmed. Junction 8E."

There is no response from the Gamma team. The data stream offers no information on their whereabouts, though I am certain they had reported earlier. They had engaged Garris. I cannot remember exactly. There are patches in the stream, incomplete strands in my memory.

I force down a shudder, and approach Neary, weapon at the ready, being sure to maintain a clear view of his face and his hands.

Confirm. Contact. Confirm. Respond.

"Neary sighted," I repeat. "Confirmed. Junction 8E."

A pause follows my subvocalization. A fraction of a fraction of a second, the time it takes me to blink, no more.

Confirmed. Revised objective. Neary. Neutralize. Confirm.

"What is the Gamma team's status," I say, daring to

break protocol.

Unknown. Last coordinates Corridor 57. Junction 3D. Revised objective. Neary. Neutralize. Confirm.

I sway where I stand, my vision blurring, the pain that the dampeners are holding at bay briefly bursting through and flooding my senses. My mouth is very dry.

"System protect us." I say the words aloud, unable to stop myself.

Neary looks up from his agonies, aware of my presence at last. There is a look in his eyes that I do not recognize, full of emotion. A thousand voices being heard at once.

"Do you smell that?" he says to me.

I discharge my weapon twice and he slumps to the ground.

"Objective achieved. Neary neutralized. Request further orders."

DISPATCH TEN

I arrive at Junction 3E and Corridor 57 and find both members of the Gamma team have been incinerated. A pulse charge at close range.

"Gamma team inactive," I subvocalize, though there is no one left to hear me. Unless Garris is somehow still connected to our internal networks without the System being aware. That seems unlikely in the extreme though. The System cannot be unaware of its component parts, even when those parts rebel against it. Garris needed to remove himself completely from the System in order to achieve his objective. I alone remain.

Revised objective. Proceed to CNS. Neutralize Intelligence. If Garris encountered, neutralize. Confirm.

I am already moving forward, following the path laid out by the data stream, as I confirm my orders.

DISPATCH ELEVEN

I encounter no resistance as I move through the internal ring. It is abandoned by all appearances. Perhaps the habitat was unmanned, the corridors and rooms vestiges of an earlier time when maintenance by humanoids had been the norm. Or maybe the Intelligence sent its humanoids out to thwart our attack, as we were sent out from the System. Somehow it did not recognize any of our teams as intruders and did not enact its defense mechanisms.

But what about Neary and Garris? Was that the defense mechanisms at play? An infection. A disturbing possibility. Unlikely, though, when incineration or a pulse charge are far more effective than relying on infiltrating the System and our data streams. We only infected the Intelligence out of necessity, with no expectation of it succeeding as it has. My path is clear and I am unchallenged, though Garris lurks beyond.

Infecting the System is inconceivable anyway. The System is greater than some mere habitat. It is no more than a collection of beings and things. The System courses through me, as true as the beating of my heart.

The smell returns, faint and untraceable. The data

stream claims otherwise, but I know it is there.

I start to move at double time, judging that I have enough reserves to maintain this pace until I arrive at the CNS and, once there, to complete my task. Garris, I assume, will be heading there as well. He knows our objective. He knows the routes the System has chosen. Interception is to be expected.

It comes as I approach the gateway to the inner sanctum, which houses the CNS, the inner and outer rings acting a shield around it.

An incendiary device goes off near my feet, forcing me to accelerate to triple time to avoid it. That is the intended effect, for as I accelerate to avoid the first blast I run straight into the second. This one a proximity pulse leveled at my head. Normally it would render me inactive immediately, severing me from the System and the data streams, but I am expecting it. A double tap explosion is standard protocol for System deployment teams.

I go inactive myself, momentarily severing my tie with the System and the data streams, shutting down all my components that the pulse is intended to disrupt and fragment. As a result, I am unconscious as I go through the pulse, my momentum carrying me through it, the automatic restart engaging once I am past.

The pulse has physical effects as well, but they are minimal, though excruciating, at least while the restart renders my dampeners and repair mechanisms inoperative. Several organs begin to shut down and I feel my body go into shock as I reawaken from inactive status.

Garris appears, materializing from the air according to my senses, though I know that is an impossibility. His knife is in his hand and at my throat.

"System be praised," he says. "Confirm. Okimba located. Confirm."

DISPATCH TWELVE

Garris' eyes are wild, his breathing loud, his voice displaying signs of the extreme duress he is under. He still believes he is working for the System. He is infected by the Intelligence.

Confirm. Contact. Confirm. Neutralize Garris. Confirm.

I can sense the rest of my systems stuttering to life, even as Garris presses his blade to my throat.

I react, the data stream and all my senses screaming at me to do so, jerking my head forward into the blade and smashing my forehead into Garris. I can feel his nose shatter beneath my blow and he takes a step back to regain his equilibrium. It is all the time I need. I have my knife in one hand and take hold of his arm with the other to keep his weapon at bay.

We fight, each of us trying to land the fatal blow. Garris has the advantage of time, for blood is streaming from my neck where his blade has punctured my throat. I will require immediate maintenance to stanch the flow.

Forty seconds to critical blood loss. Maintenance required.

The edges of my vision begin to go dark.

I wrench his arm, twisting his wrist so that his knife falls from his hand to the floor.

Thirty five seconds to critical blood loss.

He quickly seizes both my arms, fending off my attempted blows, both of us moving in a contorted frenzy.

Thirty seconds to critical blood loss.

My knees begin to feel weak and I pitch my weight forward so that he has to carry it.

Twenty five seconds to critical blood loss. Cease all activity immediately and perform maintenance.

Garris sags a bit, absorbing my weight. It gives me the space to pivot back and free one hand, allowing me to punch him hard on his shattered nose. He takes a step back and grunts in surprise.

Twenty seconds to critical blood loss. Shutdown to save vital functioning to begin in ten seconds.

I pull myself free of his grasp and bend down to pick up my weapon, leveling it at Garris.

Fifteen seconds to critical blood loss.

Garris looks at me with his wretched eyes, horrible awareness filling them.

"Do you know, we are the last?" he says, wonder in his voice. I discharge the weapon.

Ten seconds to critical blood loss. Beginning shutdown.

I override the shutdown, stanching my wound with my hand, pulling free the sealant from my emergency pouch. I barely manage to apply it before I go inactive, shutdown enforced by the System.

DISPATCH THIRTEEN

Am I the last? It does not seem possible. I struggle to recall. When were we last off vessel? When did I last see anyone other than my vessel mates? I feel a chill, spreading from my center through my extremities that the dampeners cannot contain. The smell, bitter and metallic, pervades my nostrils.

"Are there any other personnel nearby?" I query the System.

There are no known vessels.

"Who is left?" I say, this time aloud, my voice sounding small in the empty corridors.

There are no known vessels.

There is a pause in the system, lengthy this time, as though it is considering what to reveal. Ultimately it choses silence. It is my imagination, that pause, nothing more. The System is true.

Confirm. Revised objective. Proceed to CNS. Neutralize Intelligence. Confirm.

I cannot seem to get to my feet, Garris' last words haunting me. His eyes, there was something in his eyes. An awareness, awful to look upon. What did he understand at the very end?

He believed he was working for the System in attacking us, but the truth came to him in those terrible final moments. He was infected.

That is not it, I know, or not all anyway. Somehow I know this, deep in myself.

Confirm. Revised objective. Proceed to CNS. Neutralize Intelligence. Confirm.

We are the last. I get to my feet and stumble forward, confirming nothing, each corridor and junction from the schematic of the inner sanctum etched into my mind.

DISPATCH FOURTEEN

Confirm. Respond. Confirm. Revised objective. Proceed to CNS. Neutralize Intelligence. Confirm. Report. Confirm.

I do not respond, though my entire being cries out to do so. To refuse an order, to not confirm, is against the System, against all that I am. But it has to be done. I have to see for myself. I have to know.

The smell is overpowering the farther I go, a stench of corrosion and acid, and I am overcome by the sensation of it eating at my insides the more I breathe it in. The data stream tells me the air was fine, but I am no longer sure I trust it. There are more gaps in it now, fractions of a second where no information is available. Were they always there and I had somehow not noticed before? A terrifying sense of vertigo seizes me, nearly sends me falling to the ground.

Flashes of images emerge from the gaps. Silent explosions, bursts rippling across the vast emptiness. Screams that I cannot hear.

Override. Inactive. Override. Inactive...the words repeating endlessly. I try to blink them away, but my body seems unable to respond. The pain from my various wounds seems to be growing, the dampeners no longer able to compensate. I press on to the observation deck.

Confirm. Respond immediately. Confirm.

The observation deck is empty. The entire habitat is empty. What I see confirms that and more. All around the habitat are the remains of a fleet. Vessels adrift, directionless, dark as the space around them. Wreckage spiral here and there, almost invisible. I am certain I catch a glimpse of a few bodies, fully suited, adrift on that currentless sea. There is the possibility they are still in stasis, but I know they are not. I am the last.

Confirm. Respond. Confirm. Revised objective. Proceed to CNS. Neutralize Intelligence. Confirm. Report. Confirm.

"Confirm," I say aloud and turn to go.

DISPATCH FIFTEEN

I stand before the CNS of the Intelligence, wavering, barely able to stand. A cough tickles the back of my throat, the noxious scent choking me.

Confirm. Neutralize Intelligence. Final objective. Confirm.

The data stream chatters on endlessly. I ignore it, my focus entirely on the task at hand. The System is before me. The final objective. The question now is how to achieve it. The Intelligence has defense protocols in place. They may already be enacted. The agony I find myself in, the stench that will not leave my thoughts, tells me as much.

And I am so insignificant beside the System. To destroy it means destroying the entire habitat, for its tentacles are everywhere. It can reroute functions while it repairs any wounds I manage to inflict.

I am the last. I am the System. The realization brings me to my knees.

Confirm. Neutralize Intelligence. Final objective. Confirm.

Without me, what remains?

The knife is in my hands, which are damp with blood. There is a taste of tin in my mouth. Blood as well. There is something warm in my hands and I hold them up.

I look on, unblinking, as my heart goes still. The rest of my body works furiously to keep me active, the System and the data stream screaming warnings at me, all of which are futile.

Shutdown is imminent. The System will provide.

TWO SKULLS

The bones had been bleached dry by the sun and were a gleaming white amidst a sea of green grass that stretched on for miles in any direction. The sun glimmered off them, catching the eye of Harni the Cleaved, one of two riders making their way across the plain. She brought her horse to an abrupt halt, wordlessly pointing at the distant speck of white. The other rider, Mejk the Unharnessed, grunted in response and they both turned their horses toward the bones.

They came across the rest of the body in their search for the skull—a femur here, a rib there—the body obviously having been torn apart by whatever carrion hunters inhabited these parts. Mejk was forced to dismount from his horse to find the skull, which was hidden beneath an especially thick swirl of the lengthy grass. He knelt on the ground, picking it up gingerly to study it, while Harni kept her eyes watchful upon the horizon.

The skull was whole and unbroken, except for a small hole at its base where an arrow had obviously struck and killed the warrior. Mejk turned it over in his hands, counting the teeth and looking at the form of the skull with a skeptical eye. Harni interrupted his study with a grunt.

"Be quick," she said. "Someone's approaching."

"You know this can't be rushed," Mejk said, not taking his eyes from the skull.

"It may have to be," Harni said.

Hearing the urgency in her voice, Mejk looked up from the skull and cast his eyes along the horizon. "Who is it?"

"Who else," was her whispered reply.

Who else indeed. These were the Untamed Lands, which no one had claim to. But that would not stop some of the Great Tribes from doing so, especially to two warriors from the Fastarl traveling far from their lands. These plains had once been theirs in more glorious times, but that was many lifetimes ago, long before Harni or Mejk had come of age. Now the Fastarl lived upon the winds, forced to survive on their wits and at the sufferance of the Great Tribes, never to have a true home.

All that could change if Mejk was successful here . For the Untamed Lands were littered with the dead, many of them Fastarl, murdered in those dark days when the Great Tribes had driven them from their lands. And Mejk was a spirit walker. He could walk with the dead, could claim them from those places where their spirits were banished.

"Can you identify it?" Harni said, intruding upon his thoughts.

"We shall see," he said, letting his irritation show. "Have they spotted us?"

Harni nodded. "Yes. They are coming."

Mejk sighed, not looking up from the skull. Every second would be essential now. "How many?"

"Four."

A scouting party then, not a full force. A small bit of fortune this day. They would need more before it was over. First, he needed to determine which tribe this skull belonged to. All the incisors were present, but two of the molars, one on either side of the lower jaw were missing. A good sign. The forehead had been elongated by some stone binding, another positive indication. But what decided it for him were the series of thin marks along the forehead.

They could be bite marks from whatever beast had fed upon the fallen warrior, but he thought not. Too regular. He clicked his tongue in recognition. "It is of the tribe."

Among the dead on these plains were powerful warriors. The Fastarl, in the days when they had ruled all Mejk could see, had been great sorcerers, practitioners of dark arts long since forgotten by all the tribes. But not by the dead. If Mejk could walk among them, claim their spirits, he could gain the knowledge that would restore the Fastarl to their rightful place.

"Good," Harni said, her voice like a breath of wind. She was nervous, and not only because of the approaching warriors. His most difficult task lay ahead of him. Now that he had found one of their dead he had to claim its spirit.

Harni flicked her eyes from the horizon, where the scouting party continued their steady and resolute approach, and where Mejk crouched beside her in the long grass, the skull of one of their ancestors in his hand. If he was right. But he would be. For all his insufferable arrogance, Harni had to admit he was generally right about such things.

"How long?" he said, not bothering to look up at her.

She swallowed her annoyance and looked back to the approaching riders. "A span. No more."

"I have time then."

He set the skull down upon the ground, positioning it so that the barren eye sockets cast their empty gaze upon his face.

"No," she said, not bothering to hide her irritation now. "They will be here in a span."

"The Anchored One will guide me. I can bind this

one's spirit to me before they come."

"And if you don't?" she hissed. "Am I to face four riders alone?"

"I will," Mejk said, with a certainty that made her flush with anger.

Even more irritating was the fact that he would likely be able to do so and they would ride from this place without consequence. Mejk was lucky that way, everything coming to him easily. Every confrontation easily resolved, or slipped away from. Harni was not so blessed. For her, it was all a struggle, every battle a near thing.

This one would be no different. For even if Mejk succeeded in binding the spirit to him before the riders arrived, they would still have to face them. And if they had a sorcerer among them, what then? The thought made her anxious, which made her angry, and she stole another glance down at Mejk, a sharp retort on her tongue.

He was retrieving a pouch from his belt, from which he pulled forth some of the crushed sage it held and sprinkled it upon the skull. When he was satisfied there was enough he closed his eyes and began to recite the incantations.

There was no sense interrupting him now that he had begun, he would need every second. Harni looked away, back at the horizon. The riders were still approaching, but now their horses were at a gallop. Mejk would not have his span. And she would be left alone to face them.

Mejk recited the words he knew by heart, his eyes closed, letting his being slip from his body and this world and pass into the next. He knew them so well that they were automatic, a reflex, that once started there was no stopping. The journey was also familiar, the strange and unnatural sensations that assaulted his spirit serving as markers of his passage to that other world where the dead reigned.

So it came as a shock to him when Harni's gasp of surprise intruded upon his reverie, closing the passage and returning him to this world. He steadied his breath, not opening his eyes. Whatever had made Harni gasp must be inconsequential—she had not said anything, so he assumed there was not immediate danger. He tried to resume his incantation and return to the other world. But the words felt clumsy and unfamiliar on his tongue and he was a long time making his way through the folds of shadows that led to the other world.

They coalesced and dissolved, the darkness unraveling and forming again, and he had the sense that he was in a long cave burrowed deep under the earth. He began to go forward, judging by instinct and experience which pathways led from the cave to the other world above. There were those spirit walkers who became lost in this place, this half-world, neither here nor there. Their souls eventually dissipated, having no gravity to hold them together.

Mejk would not be one of those. The elders had not chosen him for nothing.

Gradually the darkness ahead took on a different hue. The shadows seemed to move away and he had a sense of form and solidity around him, where before there had been a void. A faint light shone ahead, like a moon on the wane, which gave him pause. Unlike the world he had come from, where at least two of three moons shone in the sky on any given night, there were no moon in the realm of spirits. The skies were empty and forever dark.

The pause lasted only an instant before he continued on, certain he was on the right path. The light was a distraction, one of many that assailed even the most experienced spirit walkers in this place, for the spirit world sought to claim all that entered. It was important to remain focused, both on his ultimate destination and the world of living, where Harni awaited his return.

He began to climb, the way growing steep. The light also grew brighter, though it was difficult to say whether it was coming from ahead or behind, or somewhere else.

Direction was always complex in this place. He swallowed any doubts and hurried ahead, wanting to arrive before he succumbed to uncertainty, or any other seductions that might happen to appear.

The light grew brighter and brighter, the air almost seeming warm, which he knew was impossible. He closed his eyes to steady his resolve, forcing himself forward. The light vanished, the familiar, hazy darkness of the spirit world returning. He opened his eyes and saw what appeared to be the mouth of the cave that would take him to the spirit realm.

The path to the opening was overgrown by roots, which filled him with a deep trepidation. Nothing grew here. Pressing a hand against one of the roots he discovered they were the bones of some monstrous creature interlaced together. An icy tingling stung the hand that touched the bones and he quickly withdrew it and ran ahead without heed, wanting to be as far away from the dead creature as possible.

Stumbling, and filled with a growing sense of doom, Mejk emerged from the cave to a different world.

Harni watched the riders approaching, sweat forming on her back. Her horse stirred beneath her, nickering at the sight of the newcomers. Harni's instinct was to ride as fast and as far as it would carry her. No good could come of facing four warriors, least of all in the Untamed Lands. Too many Fastarl lay in these grasses, never to rise, and she had no urge to join them.

But she could not abandon Mejk to his fate, however much she might be tempted to. It was his rashness, his certainty that had condemned her to stand alone before four warriors and protect both him and herself. But it was his ability, his incantations, and his spirit walking that might restore the Fastarl to their rightful place among the tribes. So the elders claimed. It was small comfort now that she sat upon her horse watching death ride toward her.

As the riders came nearer she saw the two in the rear had their bows strung with arrows. Harni resisted the urge to grasp the bow that was slung across her shoulder, knowing that the arrows aimed at her would sail before she could notch one of her own. Instead she rested a hand upon the handle of the obsidian blade at her belt. She did not draw it, knowing it would be a futile gesture, but hoped that it gave the appearance of fearlessness. At least it would cover the trembling in her hands.

They pulled up before her in a clatter of hoof beats and a spray of earth. The two warriors with bows drawn kept them trained upon Harni. She wondered why they were not aiming at Mejk, and stole a glance to reassure herself that he was still there and still fine. Perhaps they, correctly, identified he was no threat. Not in his current state. They would recognize a spirit walker at work.

The two others, both women rode out to confront her, their hands on their blades as well. They were all tall, half a head taller than either Mejk or her, and fearsome looking, their faces painted in red and orange hues.

Before either of them could speak, Harni announced, in a ringing voice, "We have claimed this ancestor. He is of the Fastarl."

The two were momentarily taken aback and Harni allowed herself a small instant of hope. "You have no claim to the souls in this place," one of the women said. She was oldest of the group, her breastplate lined with golden feathers. She spoke in a rasping voice, as though her tongue were trying to crawl its way from her mouth.

Harni stood her ground, clenching the haft of her blade tighter. "These are the Untamed Lands. We have as much claim to the souls here as any tribe. This one was of our people."

The women considered Harni, staring down fiercely from their horses. The silence and the stare were intended to intimidate her and to make her cede her position. Harni held her ground, refusing to betray how frightened she felt. If it came to fighting she would lose, and they knew it as well as her. Her only hope was to delay for long enough, so that Mejk could return and even the odds with his incantations.

"These lands have been ours since the lost ones left here," the woman with the rasping voice said. "We claim all that lies here, as far as the birds can fly."

Harni risked a glance at Mejk, in the fervent hope that he had succeeded in harnessing the spirit and was returning to this world. He remained in a trance, by all appearances intent upon the skull. But his eyes were rolled into the back of his head and his mouth hung open, as if he was about to speak. There was no help to be found there.

She turned back to the warriors, careful to keep her expression imperious. "We dispute your claim," she said. It was madness to threaten them when they were four and she was one, but she had no other alternative. She could only hope they thought her a spirit walker too with incantations to speak and wards in place to stop their arrows.

The woman with the rasping voice blinked, clearly surprised by Harni's escalation. She glanced at Mejk, as if suspecting a trap of some sort. He did not move and she turned back to Harni. "Very well," she said gravely.

Harni closed her eyes, but otherwise betrayed none of the fear she felt. "I demand a challenge."

For a time she was answered with silence, the only sound the wind rustling the grass across the plains. Then the woman laughed, a rasping chortle filled with spittle.

"You threaten us and demand a challenge. Why should we agree to that? How do we know you are not a spirit walker?"

"I am not," Harni said, staring straight ahead and trying not to let the quavering she felt enter her voice.

"But he is," the other woman said, gesturing at Mejk.

She was younger, with fearsome wide eyes.

"Yes," the leader rasped. "Who's to say he hasn't cast wards over both of you?"

He didn't have time and he didn't listen, Harni wanted to say. But that would give the game away entirely. The fact they did not know if wards had been cast told her none of them were spirit walkers, which leveled the ground somewhat.

"That is hardly my concern," she said, attempting a mocking smile.

The woman scowled. "I do not like this."

"Also not my concern," Harni said, her false bravado ironically filling her with confidence. She might be able to dance her way through this predicament long enough for Mejk to return from the spirit world and cast his wards.

"Fine," the woman rasped, waving a dismissive hand. "We grant you your challenge. Who among us do you wish to face?"

Mejk stared in terror upon an unfamiliar world. Somewhere he had gone very wrong. He tried to think of where it might have been, but forced the question from his mind. It did not matter where, he had been led astray. Now he had to find his way back before he was lost here forever.

What lay before him was shadow and light, substance and the ethereal. All were mixed together until he could not discern the shape or hue of anything. It felt as though he were standing atop the sky staring down at the ground. Remembering the cave from which he had emerged, he turned to retreat back the way he had come, but the opening was gone. If it had ever been there at all.

He began to mutter the incantation that would hold him to the world, to the place where his body crouched upon the tall grass that bent with the wind. Things began to feel more solid as he uttered the familiar words, even if his surroundings remained impenetrable to his senses.

These were visions, the seductions of the passage to the land of the dead, intended to waylay those, like him, who sought to enter and leave. The realm of the dead did not surrender spirits easily.

Below—or above, he still was not certain—something began to move, the formless taking form. It was a great beast taking flight, its gaping maw thrusting toward him. Mejk shuddered with fear, still repeating his incantation, telling himself that all that was here were illusions, intended to make him lose his way. He recalled the bones he had stepped across to reach here, that had stung his hand, and doubt assailed him again.

As he watched the beast approach he had an urge to cast aside his body and see what awaited the living in this desolate place. How simple it would be to surrender now, to leave Harni and his people to their pathetic fates. For that was what he both suspected and feared—all that he did in this life would be for naught. He would lie forgotten on the plains like the man whose skull he had discovered upon the grasses.

It was a seductive thought, but one which he knew he had to resist. The Fastarl needed him. He was the most powerful sorcerer among them and they had placed their fates in his hands. Even if he failed, he still had to try. He owed them that.

The terrible beast grew nearer and nearer. As it came closer, time seemed to dwindle down to a pause, everything going still. Stillness was death, of course. An end. To be resisted at all costs. Yet he could not find it in him to flee this creature. His instincts told him the way lay forward, though he was unsure whether to trust them anymore, or even which way forward lay.

The beast's maw was dripping with saliva that stank of death. It seemed to widen as it approached, promising doom. Mejk blinked, realization coursing through him, and stepped toward the mouth. The monster seemed to retreat as he approached and he began to run, racing toward the mouth as it snapped shut. He leapt through, just as the jaws closed, and found himself in darkness again.

But a familiar darkness, for he was again in the cave and his way forward was finally clear. He started to run. Time was of the essence, for every moment he remained was one in which the bonds that held his spirit to his body weakened further. This was a spirit's rightful place, the world where all spirits found their home. The world of the living was merely a way station they passed through on a journey to whatever lay beyond that horizon.

He emerged above to a plain, half-lit, though darkness reigned and the sky was vast and empty. In the far distance there was a horizon, barely glimpsed, where a darkness deeper than black resided. It beckoned to him, a final resting place. A respite from all the tribulations he had undergone. He shook his head, knowing he had to resist.

The plain held no spirits, which was not strange. No spirit would linger in a place like this, with the horizon calling them. But Mejk's incantation had been intended to call back whatever spirit had resided within the skull he knelt before in that other world. Soon enough, if he had done things correctly it would appear before him.

As he wondered where the spirit could be, a shiver of doubt passed through him. Had the incantation been malformed? Or was he somehow mistaken in his identification of the skull? If the skull had not been from a Fastarl, then the incantation would not call the spirit forth from its resting place beyond the horizon. Perhaps things had just gone wrong, as on his journey here. But things never went wrong for Mejk in this place, not once he arrived upon the dead plain.

While he pondered this mystery, a feeling of helplessness welling up within him, he heard a cry echo across the plains. It was a familiar voice and it took a moment for him to realize who it was. It was Harni, crying out in agony. Her screams had somehow traveled from the land of the living to this dead place. But Mejk was too far away to be any help now.

Harni blinked, her uncertainty returning. In a challenge, each side picked their champion. To cede that right was to say that it did not matter who was chosen, the result would be the same. Perhaps it would be. She looked at the four faces opposing her, trying to ascertain who might give her the best advantage.

They were all impossibly tall, but the women were a little shorter, so it would have to be one of them to lessen their advantage. The rasping voiced woman was much older, so Harni would be quicker. But she would have much more experience in battle, while the other woman was younger even than Harni. So which advantage did she want to be hers?

"I choose her," Harni said, pointing at the young woman.

The old woman nodded and smiled, turning to the younger woman. "Do us proud Lishj."

The younger woman smiled hungrily and leapt from her horse, handing the reins to the leader. Harni swallowed, her confidence slipping a little at the sight of the other's eagerness. Better to be cautious than overconfident, she told herself as slid from her horse and moved away from the group to face Lishj alone. The young woman followed, a sneering sort of smile upon her face and they stood across from each other and bowed. Harni offered a prayer to the gods and goddesses and drew her obsidian blade. Lishj did as well and the challenge was underway.

They circled each other, warily at first, lunging and feinting, testing the other warrior's resolve and looking for any tactical weaknesses. Lishj was very quick, but not so fast as Harni, in her judgment. That was good, because the younger woman had at least two hands' reach on her. She seemed slower moving to her left, although that could be feint intended to draw an attack from Harni.

It was Harni who attacked first, going for the left in a sudden burst. Lishj was ready for her—it had been a feint—and Harni had to dance away before she was caught by the other's blade. Her own dagger she passed from hand to hand, watching the other woman closely, deciding to let her attack to see what she would do. When it came it was a clumsy thing, easily turned aside. Harni even managed to gash Lishj in the ribs before she retreated.

First blood was drawn and Harni began to feel more confident. Lishj could defend well, but was a poor attacker and now had a wound that limited her. Harni began to methodically press her advantage, nipping in with her blade, seeking a cut here and gouge there. All with an eye to wearing her opponent down, forcing her to be constantly defending and gradually bleeding her reserves. She would weaken and eventually make a mistake that Harni could take advantage of and land a killing blow.

As Harni worked calmly and precisely against her, Lishj began to realize the doom that awaited her if she did not act. She began to launch wild attacks against Harni, which were easily repelled, and which opened her up to further assaults from the Fastarl. It was soon evident to all those upon the plain that Lishj would lose the challenge. She had cuts on her ribs and above her left breast, while her right shoulder was cut to bone and bleeding badly. Only her legs had escaped Harni's blades, and even there one of her hips had a steady trickle of blood from a narrow cut.

The time to end it was soon, Harni could tell. Her opponent was weakening, her arms slow to attack and slow to defend. But she did not hurry, staying patient and methodical, letting Lishj come to her. Letting her make the mistake.

The error she was waiting for came when Lishj lunged, a flailing arm carrying the blade coming down for Harni's head. Harni ducked within the arc of her blow, jabbing with her dagger and shoving her hard with her other hand at the same time. Lishj gasped as the knife slipped between her ribs and stumbled back from the push, tripping over her feet and falling to the ground. Harni moved in, ready to land the killing blow before Lishj could rise again.

Before she could fall upon the other woman, an arrow caught her in the shoulder. Harni screamed in agony and rage.

The rasping woman was staring in wrathful horror at the two bowmen, one of whom had an empty bow. His expression told its own story of shame, love and hate. Harni took another step forward, intending to finish Lishj off, but the bowman drew another arrow, making plain his intent.

"Are you going to allow this to stand?" Harni shouted at the others.

The rasping voice woman took a step forward, moving between Harni and her attacker, glaring at him.

He lowered his bow and returned her stare. "You are going to allow this?"

"It is a matter of honor. You know that as well as I. So does Lishj."

"I will not let her die," the young man said.

"Then you dishonor us all," the rasping voiced woman said with authority. The other bowman stood aside watching the two of them.

"Why should we let this woman of no tribe kill one of our own? I will not let Lishj die such a death out here."

Harni watched them argue, contemplating whether or not she could manage the leap to the fallen woman, who still had not risen, to finish her off before the bowman could strike. She could do so, she realized, but she would lose whatever standing the rasping voiced woman held her in and would die soon after. Her only hope lay in the woman winning this argument.

"The challenge has been set. Lishj accepted it. And now it must play out. You know this Adarn."

Adarn shook his head. "It is your folly that has led us here. There was no need to accept her challenge. If she had wards of any kind we would not be standing here. She is stalling, waiting for her spirit walker to return."

The woman sneered, moving closer to the bowman. "Is that what you think? You are so wise Adarn. Well, you do not lead us. I do. I accepted the challenge and Lishj gladly agreed to be our champion. The fight has been fair and it will end as the Gods and Goddesses intend."

"It will not," Adarn said, raising his bow and pulling the arrow tight.

"You would stain our lands with dishonored blood?" the woman said. She tried to sneer again, but there was doubt in her voice.

"These are the Untamed Lands. No one has claim to them. And no one will know what has happened here if we break a challenge. The coyotes will see to them."

Adarn and the woman locked eyes, each of them judging the resolve of the other. At last the woman nodded and stepped aside. Harni felt her heart sink and her throat was choked with rage.

"I curse you upon the blood of your ancestors," she began to say. Adarn loosed his arrow and as it struck home she began to scream again.

Harni's scream troubled Mejk deeply, but he told himself there was nothing he could do to help her. Her fate was beyond his reach, while his own grew more precarious by the moment. If the approaching warriors had attacked, as seemed likely, then it would only be a matter of time before they turned to him, or what remained of him upon the plain, kneeling on the grass before the skull. They could kill him there and banish his spirit to this world.

His concerns about that vanished as the spirit began to materialize in the air before him. The soul took shape before Mejk, shadow and dust, with hardly any form. It was a sign of an ancient being, one that had lived so long ago it barely had any ties left to its final resting place. With its appearance came a wind that stirred the grass and sent a bitter chill through him. He shuddered at it and felt a stab of terror.

His doubt returned, but he swallowed it away and prepared to bind the spirit with another incantation. He hesitated over the words, as the spirit seemed about to dissipate back into the nothingness from which it had come. Mejk silently urged it to reach out to him—to speak, to become—but it seemed unwilling. The cold breeze looked as though it might dissolve the soul back to the darkness.

But finally it did become and take something like a human form before him. There was a grimacing, shadowed face and a tall lean figure. At its belt hung two skulls that grinned mirthlessly at him. Mejk was taken aback at their sight. If this was a Fastarl he had never seen anything like him in all the souls he had summoned.

But it was an ancient being, he reminded himself, far older than any he had called forth before. That explained the difference, or at least it could. So did the power that Mejk could sense emanating from the other being. That excited him, for this was exactly what he had come for. If he could bind the spirit to him and learn his ancient magics, the Fastarl would be restored to their rightful place upon the plains.

Mejk began to speak the words of the binding incantation, knowing his time was very short, wondering if when he returned he would find Harni alive or dead. As he began to speak the spirit raised a hand and Mejk felt the words turn to dust in his mouth. He tried to speak them again, but they would not come. His tongue stumbled against his teeth and finally went still.

The cold wind returned and stung him again. Along with it came fear. This had never happened before and he could not understand it. There was only one explanation though: the spirit was using its power upon him. That was impossible, he was not of this place, its laws could not bind him. And yet it was happening.

Mejk tried again and failed to speak his incantation. Realizing that it would do no good to try again, and knowing that he had pass down through the cave to return to his body before he was killed, he released the spirit and turned to begin his journey back. As he turned to go he thought he could see the spirit smile, though when he looked again it remained expressionless, as all beings of this realm did.

Shaking his head, and telling himself he was seeing phantoms in a place of the dead, he turned to go again, starting back to where he remembered the mouth of the cave being. A strange thing happened as he did so. Though he marched in the opposite direction of the ancient being, he somehow ended up back where he had started, peering into the void of its empty eyes. He tried to go again with the same result, and again, each time with a growing urgency, heading off in a different direction. Always he returned to the same spot before the spirit.

At last Mejk was forced to admit what had occurred. The soul had bound him, just as he had bound it, and it would not relinquish its hold. This too was impossible. The souls of the dead were there to be called forth and claimed by whoever understood the incantations. A powerful spirit might slip free of even the most powerful of the spirit walkers, but they did not do any claiming themselves. It was unheard of.

Despite what Mejk's mind told him about the impossibility of what was befalling him, the being pulled him nearer and nearer. Without taking a step he was drawn ever closer to its formless shadows, and a great void, which Mejk could see hints of within its darkness. He began to struggle frantically, calling up incantations that died on his lips, trying to call forth other spirits he had bound. All to no effect.

The being smiled at him. This time there could be no mistaking it. An awful smile, full of death and misery. Mejk screamed in terror, but no sound came. As he let loose his endless, silent cry, he heard its echo in the world he had come from. Harni screamed in fear and pain, and again Mejk wondered how her voice could reach him in this place.

What is happening? he asked himself. He found himself drawn into the gaze of the ancient spirit and within its eyes he saw devastation beyond all imagining, thousands lying dead. And this being the author of their destruction.

It was only with a struggle that he pulled himself free of its terrible stare and tried to break loose. But as he did, he looked down at the two skulls at its belt and thought he recognized them. He peered closer and, with a growing horror, he recognized Harni on one side and himself on the other. A terrible laughter echoed in his ears as the darkness claimed him..

DREAM LOGIC

SHE AWOKE TO darkness, as always. A dim glow beneath her gradually expanded upwards, revealing her prone form lying upon a bed and the lines of tubes stretching up from where they entered her body to the ceiling above. Liquids of various colours and viscosities flowed up and down the tubes, an external circulatory system to complement her internal one. The dull ache, that seemed a general part of her condition in this place, returned, along with her awareness. It was strange to her this pain, because she could not feel any part of her body, beyond her head. The rest of it was numbed from whatever concoctions were being added to her bloodstream.

She had no recollection of ever having left this bed, though she must have. She must have come here, or been brought, the tubes attached and the drugs administered. There was a whole life beyond this room that was absent now that she was here. This place was a void whose current she could not escape.

A voice, disembodied and seeming to emanate from below, asked her what she had dreamed. She began to tell it.

Everyone had gone away long ago. The only ones left, besides herself, were the machines and the Fallen. The world that remained continued as it had, more or less, the systems put in place functioning after a fashion, only gradually falling into disarray. Some mutated into something else, a simulacrum of the order which had once existed. It was a shadow place now. She had known nothing else since she had begun her dreams and yet, by the dream logic which now held her mind, she knew of the older world, without having seen or experienced it.

She found herself within a metropolis without apparent end, a vast and monstrous conglomeration of structures, all in various states of decay. The largest formed rings, one atop the other, but within these rings there were other formations, some of whose shapes she could not easily define. She was a ghost upon this landscape, apart from it, moving from place to place, staying nowhere long. All her existence was a journey, adrift from any end, any goal. There was nothing to mark her passage anywhere, the only constant was the need for sustenance. Some of the machines still provided it, though they were not to be relied on as she had learned.

Her days she passed in silence, broken only by the queries of the machines that still functioned, demanding identification or asking other questions that made little sense to her. Sometimes she would respond, startling herself with the sound of her own voice, but the machines seemed not to make sense of what she said, or to ignore her as if she wasn't there. Which made sense, for she was not.

"Report."

The disembodied voice always began with this. She did not know why. Her dreams were much the same, all recognizably the same place, the same life. She was the same person in them. Why that would be she could not say. Dreams were not always like that, she knew, but then very few were made to dream as she was.

She described what she had seen as best she could, though the details always seemed to lose their focus the more she thought about them, the images slipping from her grasp. The voice always pressed her for specifics on what she had observed, as though she might be capable of analyzing the foreign world she found herself in. She could barely comprehend the place she was in now, this room and these tubes and the voice. How long had she been here? She did not trust her judgement on any of these matters.

The voice rarely spoke again once she had issued her report. This time was different though, this time it spoke again.

"Leave the premises immediately," it said. "And contact the others."

She was silent, unsure of what the voice meant. It had spoken as though she had command of her dreams, which could not be further from the truth. Things happened more or less without cause there, as near as she could discern. And what others? The Fallen? They, like her, spent their days in hiding within the ruins, though she had sometimes glimpsed them. Or were there others still, unknown to her as yet, in her dreams?

She suspected, though she had no proof one way or the other, that this fallen realm in which her dream had her trapped was underground.. Perhaps it was the ever-present shadows and darkness, the days as the nights, whole and unchanging that led to this belief. Her existence here was immutable unmarked by any sense of the passage of time. She imagined a world of caverns, hollowed out and reconstructed into this strange habitat that seemed to her without purpose. A dream within a dream, she realized, and perhaps it was just the dream state thwarting her senses and not allowing her to comprehend all that she saw.

The last words of the voice came to her mind, dimly and half-remembered, as though that were the dream and not this. She was following one of her usual trails toward a dispenser that she was knew was still working. After that, if her dream went as it normally did, she would go above to one of the higher rings where there was a large room filled with desks with screens. Some of the screens still worked, after a fashion, and she would sit and watch them flashing their information and images, until she grew restless and started moving again.

This time, compelled by the words, she continued on along the ring, chewing on the block of foul tasting food the dispenser had given her. She often felt ill after she had eaten the food, though this dispenser seemed to agree with her more than the others. It was clearly degrading, as everything here was, and part of her knew that it was only a matter of time until all the dispensers failed entirely. Would her dreams allow that to happen, would her mind compel the machines to continue to work or would the logic of situation play out as it should? And what then?

Not wanting to dwell on that, disliking the sensation of dreaming and yet aware that she was in a dream, she pressed on, ducking through corridors. Rather than taking one of her usual paths, the ones she knew were safe and abandoned, she went to those areas that the Fallen inhabited. Not all of them were nonhazardous, she knew, so she went with care, always checking each door she passed through to make sure it had not sealed behind her allowing her no escape.

One of the machines confronted her as she went, looming up out of the darkness, demanding her authorization. Its voice was disturbingly similar to the one that questioned her when she was awake, though they all sounded more or less the same. The flat monotone, parched of emotion.

"The area is contaminated. Please exit immediately.

You are not authorized."

She ignored it, ducking around its bulky frame and moving down the black corridor, the machine sounding an alarm that no longer functioned. The corridor ended at a door that was jammed, which she pushed and pried apart just enough so that she could slip through. She waited a moment to ensure it did not close on her and then turned to go further down the corridor, her path illuminated by a blinking red light along the ceiling. Was this the alarm the machine had started after her breach into his realm, she wondered, or was it from some earlier calamity?

There were a few doors off the corridor, but she knew by the shape and the markings on them that there would be nothing of interest in them. They were small rooms that had perhaps been used for storage or for those who had left to sit in and pass their days. Now they would be empty, or filled with the uninteresting refuse of the decay. At last she found what she had been looking for, a larger door than the others with symbols above its frames. It was open, its automation having failed, and she stepped through into a large chamber.

It was cavernous, the ceiling stretching up past the far reaches of her sight. There were giant tubes, fragile seeming cylinders, and pipes that curved and wound around on themselves, sheltered behind protective glass. Some glowed with dim activity while others were dark. The flashing red light was brighter here, more insistent, if that were possible. She ignored all of that, ducking around the artifacts of this previous age, looking for one of the Fallen. They would be here, she knew, the smell of them was undeniable.

After some searching she managed to find one. He leaned against one of the glowing cylinders, seeming to rest his head against it as he stared off into the distance. In spite of his faraway gaze she felt his eyes upon her, no matter where she stood as she considered her approach. At last, realizing that he would already have seen her anyway, she walked up to him directly. The heat coming from the cylinder on which he rested was tremendous. Instinctively, she crouched down as she moved forward, as though that would protect her from whatever force lay within the tube should it somehow be loosed.

Nothing happened as she came face to face with the Fallen man. The cylinder did not explode, as she had feared, nor did the man rise up and seize her. He continued to stare off into the distance, a leering grin marking his face. She eyed him warily, still unconvinced that this was not some manner of trap that he had lain for her. When he made no motion at all, after she had watched him for several minutes, she moved within range of his grasp, poised to flee at the first instant of motion.

None came and then she wondered if he were waiting for her to speak, to make plain her intentions. How did one address the Fallen? She had no idea, the machines mostly did not respond to her, perhaps it would be the same here. In this realm it seemed she had forgotten the tools of speech, though words still seemed to form as thoughts in her mind. She wet her lips and reached out to touch the man, thinking that if there were no words to speak, then this gesture might be enough.

Her hand had just brushed the cloth of his uniform when one of the machines seized her.

"You are not authorized. The area is contaminated."

The pain seemed to be worse when she awoke again. She stared at the tubes, entrapping her and allowing her this life which she led, with an innate sense of revulsion. Yet the world beyond this room was so much worse, she knew, which was why she was here. To dream. The sense of it, the logic of the task, normally so readily apparent to her, was lost in her thoughts at that moment. The pain made any thinking difficult, so much easier to lie there and exist. Let the voice guide her to the better days to come, if they were to come.

The Fallen were the dead in that nightmare from which she was never allowed to escape. She knew that, as she had not in the dream. Somehow that thought had not occurred, even as she had approached the corpse, rotted and gone mostly to bone. The bones were not white as she had imagined them to be, but a dark yellow, not unlike the smell of the body itself. They could not be the others that she had been told to find. And she had never come across anyone else in all her wanderings, aside from the machines.

The voice spoke again, insisting that she find the others. "I have tried," she said. Even the act of whispering was agonizing.

"You have failed," the voice said. "It is essential that you find the others."

"But where are they?"

"Go to the center of all things."

The center of all things, around which the rings, where she made her domain, circled, was a place she had never gone in all her journeys. Long thin corridors, barely wide enough for two people to pass through, spidered out from the rings at set intervals to the central structures of the underground metropolis. She imagined they were towers of vast height, taller even than the rings all set upon each other, stretching to the surface and beyond.

She chose one of the corridors at random, darting into the opening as though she were being watched, and then went as fast as she could manage, not wanting to spend a moment longer than she had to in this enclosed space. It was hard going, she had difficulty breathing now and there was a sharp pain in her lungs, the agony of her waking now transmuted into her dreams.

After she had gone perhaps a hundred metres down the corridor the dim red lights that illuminated the walkway no longer worked and she was forced to proceed in darkness. She went by feel, keeping a hand on the nearest wall, the only sound here her own breathing. The constant, usually unnoticed, hum that infiltrated everywhere else she had been was absent in this space. For a moment she played with the idea that she had gone into a deeper form of sleep, absent of vision and thought, but the pain and fear never left her mind, seeming to grow more present with each step she took.

As she approached what she assumed was the end of the corridor. the hum of everything crept in anew, startling her from her thoughts. There were still no lights, but even the slightest sign that some of the systems were still at work in the center of things was a comfort. A flashing light piercing the darkness in a steady rhythm foretold the corridor's end and she accelerated her pace, recognizing what it was from its silvery grey color.

The door at the corridor's end refused to open and questioned her presence there. She had expected that, from the moment the light had been visible, and she simply leaned in towards the blinking light and uttered her passkey. Her voice always surprised her in these dreams, sounding not at all as she expected, nothing like when she was awake. Now, with her breathing raspy from the pain in her lungs, it sounded harsh and dry. She swallowed, trying to work some saliva into her throat as the door responded to the key and slid noiselessly open.

The words to the key, which she used everywhere with the machines were karelia, slari, and mehara. She had no idea of their significance or how she could remember them but so little else. They had been placed there, was her theory, by those who sent her into her dreams, for this place was theirs and it followed their rules. Or perhaps it was simply the logic of all dreams, she knew what she needed to know until she didn't. She did not dwell on it, all that mattered was that the words performed as they should and she could go where she pleased.

She passed into this new and undreamt of realm, the door closing behind her as she went. The lights came alive at her entrance, brighter than any she had encountered in the rest of the buildings, and she had to clutch her head in her hands for several minutes until her eyes had adjusted. The hum of things sounded different here. It was no louder, but the pitch was somehow more pleasing to her ears. She paused to ponder that for a moment, finding the thought fruitless, and set off again in search of what she had been sent for.

Though the systems and machines seemed to be in better working order here than in the surrounding rings, there was no more sign of inhabitants. Even the fallen were absent in the rooms she looked at. Her instinctual urge was to look for another food dispenser and to see if it worked better, but she had to remind herself that such urges should be ignored in the dream state. To distract herself from her hunger, and the queasy weakness that seemed linked with the pain that now haunted this nightmare, she pressed onward from room to room, not pausing to explore as she would have in the rings, confirming only that the others were not there before moving on. The rooms themselves were uninteresting, no different than those in the rings, though in slightly better repair, with little of use to her. They showed no signs of anyone having been there in quite some time.

As she went she imagined who the others might be, what they might look like. An image came to her mind of a smooth, oval head with large unblinking eyes atop a thin-limbed, fragile body. The thing stood watching her through some screen as she went, its long bony fingers stroking the air. Light flickered at its movements and doors opened before her and others were barred so that her path was chosen. Where, she wondered, was it guiding her? It showed no emotion that she could discern as it led her, and for a moment she feared it, thinking that it was leading her toward some sort of doom. She wanted to stop, to turn back on her path and return to the rings beyond its domain.

She recovered her senses in a moment. The rings were

as dead as the fallen, she knew, she had seen them after all. The other could not be there, it must be here, and she had to be getting near. Reassured, she pressed on with a renewed fervour, the pain, which had hindered her movements and thoughts, vanishing for the moment at the thought of her quest reaching its end. On she went, her rasping breath and the smooth glide of the doors the only sound rising above the hum of the complex.

She walked for what seemed hours until exhaustion sapped her will and she longed only to sleep. The thought made her smile. As if her guide understood her condition, a door slid open beside her and she entered a large, dimly lit room. There was a console at the center and surrounding it were half a dozen smaller rooms, each open and visible to the console. Within each was a bed and what she immediately recognized as dispensers. She ran to the nearest and commanded it greedily and was delighted when it whirred into motion, darting from side to side forming a thin green rectangle.

She ate two of the bars and then lay on the bed for a moment to gather herself. When she rose to go she saw that her way was barred. A thin film distorted the air at the entrance to this inner room, which proved unyielding when she pressed against it. Her heart began to palpitate as she wondered how much air was left, even as she told herself that it did not matter, it was only a dream. She demanded that the room release her and when she received no response she began to scream and pound her fists against the field.

She was anxious when she awoke, though she could not say why. It seemed as though the room was closing in on her, the air disappearing. The tubes, the light and the voice were all the same. Her pain remained and she now rasped heavily when she breathed. Something had changed, though. For the first time since she could remember she felt imprisoned and at the mercy of unseen forces. Who was the voice, a machine no doubt, but at whose behest did it act and to what end? Why was she to dream, these endless dreams of such a desolate and broken place?

This question she said aloud to the voice with a vehemence and emotion that surprised her.

"Locate the others immediately," it said. "Leave the premises."

"Why?" she said. What could so important about them? It was a dream after all. And where was she to go to?

The voice repeated its command. When she asked why she could not leave this room now, why she had to dream these things, the answer was the same again. It was like the machines in her dream, she realized, cycling through the same series of commands, the system that compelled them long since broken, with only a few remaining fragments left to grant a semblance of order. Which meant that she was trapped here in this waking nightmare. She needed to escape, but she had no idea how, if it was even possible for her to survive disconnected from all these tubes, and if she managed to, what world awaited her beyond this one.

The center of all things, around which the rings circled, was, near as she could determine, utterly uninhabited, empty of all but the machines and herself. Unlike the rings, which were ovals atop ovals below other ovals, the central structure was rectangular, a squat block within the shadow of the outer formations. The corridors and hallways crossed at strange angles, seeming to turn back on themselves so that she was always unsure of what direction she was going. After having walked for what seemed like days, she was left with the distinct feeling that she had simply wandered in an elaborate circle, mimicking her former migrations, all to no end.

Her thoughts roamed away from this place, focusing on her waking predicament. How to escape the bonds which held her tight? There seemed no hope, especially as her sleeping and waking were reversed, with more time spent asleep, driven by nightmare, than awake. She had only moments to enact whatever feeble plan she could piece together before the tubes that fed and sustained her returned her to dormancy.

Her only hope was that she could take these convictions arrived at in her dream state, which was not quite a sleep state she knew, and carry them into her waking one. If she could do that then she would be able to rip herself free from the tubes and summon what strength and courage she had and face the terrible day. The thought of removing them made her queasy with pain. Her chest still ached, even in this place, and her breathing sounded ragged and awful. Even if it meant her death, she told herself, she would do it. Oblivion was preferable to this.

The door, when she passed it, seemed familiar and so she turned back to face it. A light blinked and a voice demanded her passkey, the door opening at her rasped words. She stepped through to a poorly lit room, only the floor lights still working. There was a console at its center and surrounding it were a half a dozen doors, which she instinctively knew led to smaller rooms. Though she was filled with trepidation, she approached each door to see if she could gain entry, driven by an unshakeable compulsion. The first four blinked and refused to budge, but the fifth slid open at her words and she passed within, the light from the floor slowly rising at her presence.

There was a bed, which she had expected, more of a chamber with a lid which sealed whoever lay within it. Attached to the lid, penetrating it at various points in fact, were tubes of all widths and colors. On the floor she could see the stained remnants of the various fluids which had once passed through them. There was also some red within, a distinct color, that could only be blood.

Her vision seemed to blur at the sight of these things, her mind going still. She could feel her hands trembling violently and her mouth forming words that she did not speak. At last she took a step forward, careful to avoid the stained floor, and put her hand on the bed. The solidity of it, the familiar texture of the sheets, made her shudder. She closed her eyes to steady herself and then opened them to look once more at the bed and the tubes extending from it up to the ceiling.

When she trusted herself, which took some time, she spoke aloud, her voice sounding very strange to her ears. "What is happening?"

The voice responded immediately. "Unknown. Widespread system failure."

"What must I do?" Her hands and legs had begun to shake again and she feared she would fall.

"Emergency protocol. Leave the premises and locate others."

She awoke to find herself sprawled on the floor near the bed, her body contorted around the stains from the fluids which had kept her alive during her incubation. Her neck ached from lying on floor, her whole body in fact was sore, her chest worst of all. She coughed and cleared her throat, ignoring the lancing pain that seized her lungs and the strange bitter taste that clung to her mouth. When she had gathered herself she rose to her feet and went into the outer room.

She sat at the console which came fitfully to life at her presence.

"Identification," it said.

"Karelia Slari Mehara," she said and was granted access. "System update."

She half-listened as the console updated the various system functions, thinking instead of her days spent wandering this ruined place, her mind nearly as damaged as it was. How had she come to be in that state? She could not remember and she had no idea what had occurred here. It was all lost to her.

When the update was finished she left the room, heading down a series of hallways that led to what was, according to the console, one of the last functioning lifts. She needed medical attention desperately, she knew, but from what she could gather from the console, the medical systems were broken beyond her ability to repair. Her only hope lay elsewhere.

The lift took her to the top of the central unit where she knew the main command center was located. Her only hope was that enough was still working there that she could manage a distress beacon of some sort. The lift lurched slightly and a strained vibration began to sound at her feet. For a terrifying moment she thought it was going to seize up and leave her stranded somewhere between levels. It kept ascending, though moving slower, the vibrations growing louder. The heat became noticeable as well and she was unable to stop various doom laden scenarios from racing through her mind.

When the lift reached its final destination, lurching to a halt, the door did not open. As she tried to control her breathing and still her panic she punched one of the lift buttons. It had the desired effect and the lift door opened slowly, grinding against its tracks. She ran out before it was even fully open, catching her knee on one of the panels, not even noticing what she was fleeing into. It was an anonymous darkened corridor that gradually flickered to something resembling light. After gathering her bearings and steadying the rasp of her breathing, she set off to the left. The first door she came to she gave her name to and entered.

Karelia gasped. Above, all around, were the stars. She looked on in amazement, her heart pounding, a kind of vertigo seizing her. The lights came to life fitfully at her feet, revealing the command stations. She stepped towards the nearest and a voice asked for her name.

THE BURNED ONE

1

It was in a tiny corner of what was once the Austro-Hungarian Empire, near its southern extremities where conflict with its Ottoman neighbor was a constant, and where all the many blessings of modernity brought by the nineteenth century had yet to make their way, that the stories of the Burned One became a part of the local folklore. The origins of the tales are obscure. Few in these, even more modern times, can be found who can recall having heard them. In time, they will be available (if at all) only in the archives of the folklorists and anthropologists, who happened to find themselves in one of the five or six villages in the valley south of the Rudenka Mountains, two days journey north of the Danube.

I am here to record that I was one, though more an amateur than a true scholar. Not only that, I met the man himself in those mountains. Such a thing seems impossible as I write it now, but it is true. My memory has not failed. I have not gone mad or surrendered to hysteria. I am of sound mind and body, and the events that I recount here did, in fact, actually take place.

How strange a thing to be writing again after such an interval of years. I was a different person then than the one who puts pen to paper now. What compels me to return to it, after so long, I cannot say. So many things have changed, and so much has been lost in my lifetime, but perhaps I can save this small piece.

It was between the two terrible wars that consumed so many lives—my own included, though that was later—that I found myself in the remnants of that once vast empire. How I came to be there is a tale of its own. After the Great War, my elder brother Frederick returned a broken shell of a man and I endeavored to care for him as best I could. Our parents did not survive the war, though the conflict never touched them. They perished in a motor accident.

The effort to care for my brother was more than I could manage, though I persisted until I was left nearly as damaged in my mental state as he. I sacrificed my own life for his lost one, not marrying, though I had suitors, and we became more and more reclusive in our ways. Finally, the doctors intervened and recommended that I leave Frederick to their care and take a vacation to restore my fallen spirits.

They recommended a Mediterranean stay—sea air and villas, wine and recuperation—but I have never been one for that. I took a steamer to the Adriatic, travelling from Trieste to Kotor and then inland to Cetinje. From that moment the region never left me and I returned many times, going further and further into those areas where the borders were unsettled, or where the villages were so isolated that it was almost as if the previous century had not ended. Everywhere I went I collected the stories of the place, talking to the locals until they were annoyed by my prying. It was in this way that I came across the first whispers of the Burned One.

It was said he had lived in the Rudenka Mountains, descended from a long line of nobles of indeterminate origins. Some said Hungarian, others Romanian, others still Turkish. Conquerors all, in that valley. The old ways were still in place there, for it was cut off from the rest of the empire, from that beacon of civilization Vienna, even from Budapest and Bucharest. Ancient forms of tribute were still demanded by the lords of the place. The firstborn child of the year, from each of the villages, male or female, was to be given to the noble family, upon the day they turned five.

Such a barbaric practice could scarcely be imagined, and yet, when I spoke to others throughout the region, it was common practice for a time. Only in this particular valley, it seems, did it persist, far longer than it should have. Still, there were few complaints about the custom, as is often the case when customs are observed, for the children, though stolen from their parents, were given a good life. They managed the nobles' estates, cared for their children, and became their soldiers. All that changed with the Burned One.

He too demanded the firstborn tribute, but the children did not become his servants. In fact, he dismissed all the staff who worked on his estates, letting the land return to forest. He abandoned all his family's ancestral homes but one, a castle deep within the Rudenka Mountains, high atop a cliff, vast and impregnable, overlooking the whole valley. It was there he demanded the tribute be brought, threatening to unleash devastation upon the villagers below if they failed in their task.

For many years they continued to do so, though they knew the Burned One was quite mad. Their fear was too great and they could see no way to escape his considerable wrath. It was said he was well-versed in alchemy and other forms of magic, and had built an army of automata to serve him. And he had all those children already sent to him, though what became of them no one knew.

Here the stories varied. Some said that he was using them for some strange alchemical rites that harvested their souls. While others declared that he had not constructed automata, but instead had turned the children into them, hypnotizing them and compelling them to all manner of horrific deeds. Others still said that he sacrificed them to whatever infernal gods he worshiped.

All agreed on how the tribute ended. A hero from a foreign land—there was no clear agreement on which—arrived and heard the sorry tale of the lost children and the tribute to the madman and determined to set things right. The woman—the stories were all very clear on this point—journeyed up to the castle alone to confront the Burned One. In some versions, she tricked him into releasing the children from his magical bonds. Once the spell was broken he had no power in the land and vanished. In others, the Burned One fell in love with her at first sight and the woman traded herself for the release of the children and the end of the tribute.

These tales, which I heard dozens of times, with even more variations than I have recounted here, fascinated me to no end. I had intended to spend only a day in the valley, but I found myself staying longer and longer, going from village to village, and house to house, asking to hear the tale again. Something about it disturbed me and yet also compelled me to discover more.

Perhaps it was the villages themselves that accounted for my attraction, for they were quite different from those I had encountered elsewhere. Not only were they isolated and seeming apart from time, as though the world had continued on while they remained still, they were oddly quiet. There was none of the usual clamor of a habitation, with children running to and fro at play. The dogs did not bark and even the birds seemed somber in their songs. Yet the inhabitants were hardly doleful themselves. They welcomed me to their homes with pride and good cheer, and gladly answered the multitude of questions I had.

Foremost among them was why the man was referred to as the Burned One. Here again the stories varied. All agreed that his face was badly scarred from burns, but disagreed as to their provenance. Some said he had been born with the scars, that his mother had been cast into a pit of hell by his father, who had come to realize the monster within. In other versions, the mother or the father, or both, tried to kill the child by burning him, only to fail in the attempt, either because their compassion would not allow them to go through with such a terrible deed, or flames alone could not kill the child.

Every time someone told me the tale, they would conclude by saying the castle still stood in the mountains and I could visit it if I liked. No one from the villages had been there in quite some time, for the noble family's line had died out with the Burned One and the castle had been abandoned. The only ones who knew the way were the shepherds who took their flocks into the mountains when the snows receded, and it was one of them who agreed to take me there.

It was just after the summer solstice, and the pagan influenced celebrations that went along with it, when I was taken up from the valley into the mountains. My guide was a man of middling years I would hazard—though he seemed ageless, neither old nor young, as so many of the villagers there did. The shepherd whistled as he led me up the road, going at a steady pace. The day was warm, but as we ascended higher and higher the air turned cool and I had to put on a jacket.

It was evident that the trail we walked upon had once been part of a broader passage through the mountains, though it had long since been overgrown. Now it was simply a path for sheep and the men who watched them. The higher we rose the less distinct the way became and the more I began to suspect the kindly shepherd had led me astray for some foul purpose. It was only later that I realized how right I had been.

After some hours of ever more arduous climbing, we arrived upon a ridge that looked over the entire valley and I saw a castle perched upon its far end. It seemed to loom over the surrounding mountains and the valley below.

Once I descended again I felt its presence everywhere I went, as though the Burned One was watching over his subjects from beyond the grave.

The shepherd gestured toward the castle, indicating the way across what looked like treacherous ground. He would go no further.

2

For some reason, I had expected something gothic and baroque, full of spires and chiaroscuro effects, but the castle was far more ancient than that. It appeared to have been carved from the mountain itself, stern and forbidding, with no ostentation. That, at least, was its outer appearance, but it proved to be deceptive once I passed through the broken gate. Within I found a baroque masterpiece, ostentatious and overwhelming. Each wall seemed to have some form of ornamentation, whether plaster, wood or marble, while the ceilings all had magnificent frescos, painted by some forgotten master. It was as though all the seventeenth and eighteenth centuries of Europe had been collected into one place.

It left me breathless as I wandered through the seemingly endless corridors and rooms. I do not recall how long it was before it dawned on me that the castle was not a ruin, as its outer walls suggested. The ornamentation was intact, the frescos undamaged, all of it seemingly untouched by vermin, weather or time. Aside from a healthy layer of dust, there was nothing to suggest the castle had not been inhabited for over a century.

Had someone been living here all this time?

It seemed impossible to credit. Someone in the villages below would have been aware. The shepherds would have seen the smoke from the fireplaces. Servants would have come and gone. Food and drink would have come from somewhere. A person could not simply live, without leaving some traces for others to see. Some signs would have been evident. And yet, the more I wandered through the corridors, pulled deeper and deeper within, the more certain I became that the castle was inhabited. But by who?

Despite the surety of my feelings, I could find no further signs of habitation. I was about to abandon my search and leave to find the shepherd, so that I might return to the villages below, when I came across a room with a closed door. It drew my immediate attention, for most of the rooms had been either lacking in doors or they had been left open.

I tried the handle and found the door locked. A chill went through my body and I quickly withdrew down the hallway, casting a glance back as though I might have awoken some long slumbering beast. Though I wanted to flee further, I remained, my curiosity overcoming my trepidation. I was compelled to see through the journey I had begun all those years ago at the behest of my doctors. This moment seemed to be the culmination of all this time spent in these foreign regions that now felt more my home than my own.

The door opened and a man emerged from within. I was left both astonished and unsurprised at the sight of him. He was dressed in the attire of another age, with an elaborately embroidered velvet coat and waistcoat. His breeches were tight and extended to his knee and shoes were leather, with the most ornate buckles I have ever seen. On his head was a powdered wig, the hair extending just past his ears.

All of that was arresting enough, leading me to wonder if I had by some magic stepped back through time into another age. But most unsettling of all was the mask upon his face. It was wrought from iron, or some other metal, carefully crafted to match the contours of his face and rested there, seemingly without other attachment. There were holes carved for his mouth, eyes and nostrils. It was, in many ways, a face made metal and as fine a craftsmanship as I had ever seen.

That was not what disturbed me, though. It was the thought of what lay hidden beneath. For it seemed the stories I had taken to be mere folk tales, elaborated on until little of the real remained, were in fact true. More than that, the Burned One somehow lived still.

"Welcome," the Burned One said. His voice, deep and sonorous, did not sound muffled behind the mask. "It has been so long since someone has come looking for me."

"How are you still alive? It has been…" I was unable to finish the thought.

I sensed, rather than saw, the smile that formed beneath the mask. "Centuries. Yes. Once, I received luminaries from across the empire. Scientists and philosophers who wanted to study my methods. But that all ended some time ago."

"The empire is gone as well."

He shrugged, as though such matters were of no consequence. How could they be to one apparently immortal?

"We have always been isolated here. And people have such poor memories. They forget."

"They have not forgotten you below. There are stories…" Again I could not find the words. If there was any truth at all to the stories, and now I had to believe that there was more than some truth, then I dared not risk incurring this strange and awful man's wrath.

"They would not," he said and gestured for me to follow him into the room he had emerged from.

It was a gesture of command and I followed instinctively, in spite of my growing fear. The room into which I stepped had once been a hall for banquets or receptions, but the Burned One had converted it into his home within the castle. There was a bed and several wardrobes containing all his clothes, as well as chairs and couches for him to take his leisure. A vast array of equipment was spread about on various tables, and I saw what appeared to be experiments that he was conducting—whether of chemistry or alchemy I knew not enough to say. The walls were lined with shelf upon shelf of books. Those multitudes left me in awe, and for a moment I forgot the strange man who had beckoned me and hurried to peer through some of them. I saw obscure histories and philosophical treatises, forgotten religious tracts, and alchemical texts from the Renaissance, among others.

At last I forced myself to turn and face the Burned One. He had been watching me and now gestured for me to sit opposite him in one of the ornate high-backed chairs in the room. Though it looked torturous, it was quite comfortable and I felt slightly more at ease.

The Burned One studied me from his chair, a finger resting lightly upon his mask. He made no move to speak, which left me uneasy. I could not stop thinking of the stories I had heard. How he had been vanquished by a lone woman who had gone to confront him in this castle. Was I somehow the woman of that tale? Was I to be the villagers' savior? It seemed too incredible to even consider, and yet I found myself contemplating it.

When it became clear the Burned One was not going to speak, I endeavored to quiet my own fears. "How is it that you are still alive, after all these centuries?"

"Surely you have heard the tales," he said, nodding in the direction of the valley below.

"Some, yes," I said. "That is why I came here, in point of fact. I was curious to see what relation these rather fantastic stories had with reality. Or at least what remained of it."

"This is what remains." Again I could sense his smile.

"The tales have some truth in them, to be sure. To be sure. More than you believe, I think, though not in the manner you would expect."

Again I quailed at the thought that those poor villagers might see me as some sort of savior from the fiendish tribute they were enslaved by. Yet, they had not seemed subjugated. There had been no anguish or horror in their recounting of the tales of their former servitude. And it had clearly been a past they spoke of, not one they had lived. There was no tribute now. Perhaps there never had been. This strange man, who apparently had lived for centuries by some unknown mechanism, had no hold upon their collective minds, except as a terrifying story to tell children or strangers.

I felt more at ease now. Who was to say if this man truly was the Burned One? He wore a mask, and claimed to have lived for centuries, but offered no proof otherwise. He may have simply been some vagrant from one of the villages below who had come to claim the castle and restored this room as his residence. That did not explain the relatively pristine state of the rest of the castle, but I now felt confident that there was some other, more rational explanation for it. Perhaps the Burned One had not been the last of his line—surely some cousin, however distant had survived and inherited the place, only abandoning it after the war and the fall of the empire.

"What parts of the tale are true?" I said, being sure to put all the doubt I could muster into my voice.

"The tribute, of course," the man said. "Though it was not a tribute exactly. It was a price they paid. The rest of the tale was concocted to assuage their guilt over what had been done. I require no such disguise. I understood the cost and paid it gladly. You will too in the end."

I blinked, not yet willing to comprehend what he had said, my fear of being the unchosen savior of the villagers returning afresh. Did he expect me lie with him? To sacrifice my life so that their children might be freed?

He cannot be the Burned One, I had to remind myself, *he is just some charlatan trying to outwit you.*

I took a steadying breath. "What price was that?"

It was his turn to be taken aback. He leaned forward imperceptibly, as if he had misread me earlier and wanted to study me closer now. "Why the children, of course."

I felt my hands begin to tremble and buried them in my lap. "They told me the tribute had ended."

"It did, over two hundred years ago. The children were given to me and there have been no more since."

I thought I had somehow misunderstood the Burned One, but gradually I came to realize I had not. With a rising horror, I tried to recall if I had seen any children in any of the villages. Surely I had encountered one somewhere. But the more I thought about it, the more I came to realize I had not. There had been no children underfoot in any of the homes, no children running about on the streets, or working in the fields, no schools of any sort. How had I missed so odd and obvious a fact? My only explanation is that, because my circumstances had not allowed for thoughts of children—to say nothing of my ill and childless sibling—I gave no thought to their absence, for they had always been absent from my life. It was simply normal.

Another thought occurred to me, leaving me ill. "They are still here?" What cavern in the hidden depths of this castle had he hidden them in? And to what purpose? It was unfathomable.

"They have long since passed to their maker," the Burned One said. "Theirs was a noble sacrifice."

"What was gained by their murder?" I asked the question, even as I knew the answer, knew it with a certainty that terrified me.

"Eternity."

"How could you? How could they?" I was on my feet without my even realizing it, backing toward the door.

"Would you not sacrifice a life for eternity? Is it not a

93

worthy trade off?"

"It is against all nature." My revulsion and emotion was such that there were tears in my eyes. I fumbled at the door, wanting only to escape this castle, these mountains, this valley, this terrible place.

"They were sacrificed so that others might live on. Is that not the way of the world?"

"It is a cruel inversion of the natural order. They were the future. Not you, your time has passed." In spite of myself I stayed, my face hot with my growing fury at the indifference of this monster.

"The natural order is cruel and avaricious. Here I have maintained and cultivated a civilized order, an equilibrium that has existed for hundreds of years. We who live here are better for it. Is there any murder below, any of the madness that has touched the rest of this sorry continent these last years? There is not."

"But the price," I said. "Those children. Nothing is worth those children."

"They struggled with it, as you struggle. But they came to understand that, in the end, it was worth the price paid. You will too."

I did not wait to hear any more. I fled from the room and from the castle, not bothering to find the shepherd to guide me below. Even though it was approaching nightfall by the time I made it into the valley, I hired someone to take me by carriage from it that very day, swearing I would not spend another instant in that awful place.

3

In the intervening years, my thoughts would often return to the castle atio the Rudenka Mountains and the villages it overlooked. My dreams were often haunted by visions of the Burned One removing his mask to reveal a visage so horrific I perished at the sight of it. While I wrote and published many of the folk tales I collected on my journeys, and even attempted some anthropological articles on the subject, I avoided all mention of the villages beneath the Rudenka Mountains.

I told myself that these were ancient wrongs that had survived against all odds into our modern present, that the sadistic and tribal ways of that corner of Europe were as much a cause as any peculiar madness the Burned One no doubt possessed. Events proved me wrong, for in the decade following my encounter with the Burned One, savage new ideologies rose to prominence, leaving blood and despair in their wake.

My family and I were swept up in the war that followed. Though the Great War had seemed all consuming, Hitler, and the uncivilized hordes who followed him, truly consumed all in their path. Europe and its great empires were all vanquished and I, the daughter of one such, was left only with ruins. Worse, I was left alone, for my brother had perished during our flight from the path of the Nazis.

As the war ended and the killing zones began to quiet, I was faced with an existence without purpose. All that I had put my faith in, all my endeavors, seemed for naught. What civilization was there in Europe? None remained that I could see. There was only the mask of civility that was badly settled upon the barbarous faces that stared across the new Maginot line the great powers drew across Europe. I had no faith in communists, they sought only destruction, not order. And the Americans were no better in their way. What culture, what birthright, did they possess to rule the world as they so evidently desired?

The idea of returning to my ancestral home at the war's conclusion filled me with utter despair. The place seemed dead to me. I felt as though I stood upon a great precipice, staring down at a vast abyss of nothingness, all that remained of the world that was mine. My thoughts were deeply troubled. If all that civilization had built could be cast asunder by a few madmen, all that I had accomplished turned to dust, what purpose was there to any of it?

I could find none, especially not on the ruins of my estate. I had no strength remaining to build something anew. Instead, I found myself thinking more and more of the Burned One and his valley of the eternal living. Had they survived the depredations that seemed to have touched every corner of the continent? It seemed impossible; the dark forces that had consumed the continent had touched everyone's lives in some way.

After a year of aimless existence I determined to return to the mountains and the valley and see what remained of his immortal works. I left in spring, telling no one—there being no one left who I wished to keep informed—and followed the same route I had taken in an earlier lifetime to reach the Rudenka Mountains. Those lands now lay under the Marxist thumb, and it required some ingenuity and the last that remained of my family's valuables to cross the necessary borders.

I arrived in the valley as night crept across the sky utterly exhausted, and yet I still roused the locals from their homes until I found someone who would guide me up the mountains to the Burned One's castle. Many protested and refused, saying the path was far too dangerous to travel so late at night. A shepherd finally volunteered and, as I peered at him closely through the growing shadows, I felt certain he was the same man who had guided me up before. If he had aged at all, I could not tell.

As we made our way up into the mountains—the path muddy and still snow-covered at some points—we talked of the war and the new order that had followed it. The shepherd professed not to care much of these events. "Such things don't bother us here. We go on as we always have."

"And what of the Burned One? Is he still there?"

The shepherd looked at me confused. "He has been dead for centuries. You remember the stories."

I felt a chill run through me. Who had I encountered that day, all those many years ago, if not the Burned One? The rest of our journey passed in silence as we climbed higher and higher, the lanterns we carried providing barely enough light to guide our steps along the precipitous trail. We arrived at the ridge upon which the castle sat and again the shepherd would go no further, only indicating the way for me to go.

Something about his gesture struck me and I turned to peer at him through the gloom. "You brought me up here before. Do you remember?"

The shepherd nodded. "Of course, ma'am."

"You don't look a day older than the last time I saw you," I said.

"You're too kind, ma'am. It's the poor light tricking you."

I shook my head. "I think not. You've been in this valley over two hundred years, haven't you?"

The shepherd did not answer, his gaze never breaking from mine.

"Was it worth the sacrifice?"

"It was not I who made the sacrifice," the shepherd said. "But I expect they thought it worth the cost. They authored us, after all."

He gave an awkward little bow and turned to amble down the trail. I almost called out to him, wanting an explanation of those final words, but I hesitated and he was lost to the darkness. *They authored us.* What exactly had he meant by that?

I had no time to give it any further thought, for the darkness was growing and the way to the castle was treacherous. Holding my lantern up high, I hurried on.

The castle appeared unchanged by the intervening years. There was still a layer of dust over everything, but otherwise everything remained as it was. The frescos and ornamentation were still as magnificent as I recalled them being, even under the feeble light of my lantern. By memory, I returned to the locked door where I had found the Burned One. I found it closed and knocked upon it, the sound echoing down the hallway.

For a long time there was no response and I began to fear the entire trip had been for naught. Just as I was preparing to abandon my quest and return to the valley, I heard soft footsteps approaching the other side of the door. The lock slid away and the door opened and I was brought face to face with the masked one again. He blinked at me from behind it and motioned me within without a word, moving slowly, as if he had just awoken from a deep slumber.

The room itself was precisely how it had been before. My memory for such things is better now than it was, but I am certain of this. Every detail of that first meeting was etched upon my mind and I found myself wondering if I was dreaming somehow, so unchanged was everything. Had the Burned One moved in all the time I had been gone? Or were his days so ordered that no entropy of any kind entered his domain?

After taking in the room in a kind of daze, I sat opposite the Burned One. He set a finger lightly upon his metal chin as he studied me.

"You have returned. You are first in a long while to do so. Once the great minds of Europe called upon me to witness my works."

"So you said before." I could hardly contain my excitement, though I could not have said why I should feel so when my previous encounter had filled me with horror.

"I have done everything before and will do everything again, or so it seems. You have rethought the cost incurred, I see."

"What makes you say that?" I replied, parrying for time. In truth I had. I desperately wanted the solidity of existence, unaffected by the passage of years and the depredations of humanity, that he seemed to offer. But I could not trust him. Not entirely. Not yet.

"You would not be here otherwise. No one returns unless they are willing to undergo the sacrifice necessary."

"I have no child to offer you. No kin of any kind," I said. "Nor would I, even if I did."

"You have yourself to offer, that is all that is required."

"But what did you require the children for? Was it just for your pleasure? Am I to be just for your pleasure as well?"

"They were sacrificed it is true. As was the Burned One himself. We are what remains."

He reached up and pulled off his mask, making visible a hole in his head around his eye. Where bone and other matter should have been there was only something vaguely metallic and mechanical that my brain could not quite comprehend. I felt an immediate sense of revulsion, followed by extreme curiosity. What was he exactly? How had he been made? Whose creation was he?

He returned the mask before I had a chance to study his visage more closely. "The Burned One authored me, just as the tributes authored their immortality. I can do the same for you."

A part of me wanted to flee in that moment, to return back down the mountain as I had that first day. But I stayed in my chair, sitting across from the Burned One. Even now, I still think of him as such. He both was and was not. In that moment I truly understood the price paid and its worth. I would be both lost and saved in the same instant. I would perish and yet survive.

To what end? I have yet to find the answer.

QUARANTINE PROTOCOL

THE DAY HAD BEEN humid and now the sky, with its gathering clouds, promised a storm. The glasses of beer Marta had poured for them both had glistening pools of water at their base. She called to Jon from the patio that overlooked the courtyard in their apartment complex, "Are you coming out?"

"Yes," he said and in a moment he joined her. They sat for awhile in a peaceful, easy silence, drinking their beer and looking at the sky.

"Might be a storm tonight," Jon said.

"I hope so."

Jon smiled. Marta had always disliked the heat of the summer and the humidity that came with it. She enjoyed the drama of the storms as well, the way the air went still before they arrived and then the abrupt and torrential rains, along with the cataclysms of thunder and lightning. It was these simple pleasures that they clung to when so many others were denied them now.

"Are you going out tomorrow?" he asked her.

"Yes, I have to get my prescription."

He nodded and they both lapsed into silence, this time marked by a shared unease, which lasted until the beers

102

were gone and they went back inside.

Marta left first thing in the morning, the sun still hidden behind the city's skyline. The streets were nearly empty, with only the odd car driving past her. Most of them were official vehicles, Quarantine Patrol or the police, making their daily circuits. There was one civilian vehicle that drove alongside her for a moment, causing her to stop and watch as it continued down the street for a few blocks before turning onto a main thoroughfare. It was such a rare sight that she was immediately suspicious of the driver's intentions. She had a hand radio with her, tuned to the Quarantine Patrol channel, but she decided against using it and wasting the battery.

There were few other people about, all of them alone and wary like her. Their encounters always followed the same elaborate dance, with one person moving across to the opposite side of the street so that they could pass by each other without risk. Proximity led to contamination, those were the watchwords of all their days. One could never be sure who had escaped the Quarantine Patrol and was wandering the streets polluted, which was why people rarely left their homes.

In many ways, she reflected, because so few people were ever about it was far safer to move around the city now than in the first weeks after the contamination had arrived and people had been more or less unsuspecting. The mechanism by which the disease spread had been unclear then – it was still poorly understood now, as far as she knew – and governments, in an attempt to calm their populaces had emphasized the need to carry on with daily life, with the usual flu-related precautions taken. Washing hands, coughing into sleeves, staying home if you felt ill. None of these had been effective in least, for the contamination moved seemingly at whim from person to person.

Proximity to others increased ones chances

exponentially, as had been shown by the terrible events of the first months of the contamination when the whole world had been awash and overwhelmed by the disease. It was soon very easy to avoid people, for the contamination spread at an alarming pace and the mortality rate of those who contracted it was 100 percent. Whole cities, whole countries, had essentially been wiped from existence in a matter of weeks. The upheavals that had inevitably followed, the panic and riots and government overthrows, had only exacerbated the problems and hindered a search for a cure. Only in a few places had the institutions responded and imposed the Quarantine Protocols upon their populaces, which had slowed the spread of the disease, buying time, though for what no one was quite sure.

A police car, now emblazoned with the markings of the Quarantine Patrol, pulled up beside her, it's lights flashing. Within she could see the two officers in their biohazard gear, both studying her warily, neither making a move to leave the vehicle . One spoke into the radio and asked for her name.

"Marta Gilovic," she said, being sure to keep her voice even and calm, fighting down the panic she always felt in these situations under the suspicious gaze of the authorities. Her expression, she hoped, was placid, showing no marks of the violent emotional surges that would overtake victims of the contamination. These were the first symptoms that the Quarantine Patrol looked for and any display of them would result in someone being placed under quarantine until the contamination manifested itself.

"Residence?" the officer asked. She answered, though they would already have the information once they had put her name in their computer. All the uncontaminated had been entered into the Protocol's database and were checked on regularly and updated.

"Living with?"

"Jon Lewmach."

"His condition?"

"He is uncontaminated."

"Reason for being out?"

"My prescription needs filling."

There was a pause as both officers frowned. "I see no conditions listed here," one of them said finally.

To limit people's contact with each other the Quarantine Patrol arranged all deliveries of food and medicine to the residences of the remaining uncontaminated. Only those who worked in essential services were allowed to go to work or congregate and they were issued biohazard gear. Marta had worked downtown in an office and for a time, after the Protocol had been instituted, she had worked from home, until too many of her co-workers had perished and the company had ceased to exist. Now, she awaited reassignment to a new position within the Protocol. Jon had started making deliveries every other week, soon it would be full time. In the meantime, they were not supposed to leave their homes except in emergencies, although some leeway was granted. It was understood that one could not simply be expected to spend every waking hour in their homes.

"It's an elective prescription," she said and saw the frowns of the officers deepen.

She was certain they were going to insist that she return home. It was within their power. The unpolluted had to be protected after all, at all costs. An overwhelming sense of desperation threatened to well up within her and she fought to keep those clouds from her face. She had to get her prescription refilled, no matter what the Quarantine Protocol might say, it was essential to her. Enough to risk her life over, and it was hers to risk in the end, no matter what the officers might say. A shared look between them told her that a decision had been made and she breathed a sigh of relief as they drove away without a word.

It was twenty-five blocks to her destination, fifteen north and ten west, right through the heart of what had once been downtown. It was an eery and empty place now, the power cut long ago, to conserve what remained. The power grid and other major infrastructure still functioned to a degree, though for how long was anyone's guess with fewer and fewer people left to maintain it. They only had electricity in the evenings and only in the few neighborhoods of the city where the Quarantine Protocol remained in effect. Contaminated zones, like downtown, had been abandoned by the Protocol, though not by everyone.

The high rise looked like any other on the block. There was a restaurant and a pharmacy on the main floor, some offices and a skywalk connecting to the building across the street on the second. Above that were more offices and above that apartments. All of downtown had been emptied by the Quarantine Protocol, but those who could not live under that law had returned, here and elsewhere. The spray painted red X's signified that it was still inhabited. Here was where one could find all those things deemed inessential by the Protocol.

She passed by the elevator and headed for the stairwell and began to climb the fifteen flights, the flashlight she had her only guide. It was stuffy and hot and sweat was soon running down her face. As she went a door opened and then clanged shut above her as someone began to descend. They halted upon hearing her footsteps. Marta continued on to the top of the next flight and then called out the floor number to the person above, exiting the stairwell and moving well back of the doorway to wait. After a few minutes there was a loud knock at the door. She waited at least a minute more before renewing her ascent.

When she reached the fifteenth floor she knocked loudly and then waited before entering. She moved quickly down the hallway until she reached Apartment 1543.

Hanging on the doorway was a clipboard from which dangled a pen. Taking up the pen she wrote down what she needed and what she had to offer and then knocked on the door. She turned and walked back the way she had come until she reached Apartment 1522, which she entered after knocking to ensure it was empty.

The apartment had all the furniture from its last occupants. There were even magazines and letters from months ago sitting on one of the tables. She had long ago stopped looking at such markers of the disappeared. Instead she went to one of the windows, peering through the closed drapes to look at the streets below. She could see a man passing near the entrance of the building walking erratically and her mouth went dry. Though she urged him on he sat down on the sidewalk right near the entrance. As she pondered how to avoid the polluted man when she left there was a loud knock two doors down from the apartment she was in.

When she had counted off thirty seconds, Marta left the 1522 and went down two doors. Unlike the other, Apartment 1526 was completely empty with light streaming in from the drapeless window. In the center of what would have been the living room there were several small boxes. Seeing them she could not contain herself and she ran forward, dropping to her knees to inspect them. She opened each one to inspect the pills, ensuring they were all still within their plastic casing. That done she popped one of them free and, with a shaking hand, swallowed it. The boxes she put in her bag exchanging them for a small container of strawberries that she had picked that morning from the terrace garden of their building.

The contaminated man was still sitting at the entrance when she had descended to the fourth floor. There was another entrance on the opposite side of the building but even that, she feared, might be too close to the contamination. Instead she decided to take the skywalk, though it was a journey into the unknown. That building had been unmarked, meaning it was abandoned. In her experience the polluted were drawn to people, the internal logic of the disease insisting that it be spread, so an empty building would likely be safer than chancing the other entrance.

Her decision made she did not linger. It was never good to remain away from where the Protocol was in force. The uncontaminated in these areas lived on the knife's edge and preferred it that way, if the reports of beatings and theft and worse that were broadcast were true. She did not doubt it, not after surviving these last months where any illusions about what people, contaminated or not, were capable of had been shattered utterly.

Marta moved quickly across the skywalk, feeling exposed for some reason in the glass walkway. The high rise she entered was much the same as the other one, filled with abandoned shops and stands, all draped in shadows, daylight rising up from the entryway below to guide her. A series of frozen escalators led down to the main floor. She stood atop one, peering around the lobby to ensure she was alone before starting down. The escalators emptied out toward three revolving glass doors that glimmered where the sunlight caught them. What she could see of the street beyond appeared empty but she walked from one end of the lobby to the other to confirm that there was no one near before stepping into the nearest revolving door.

The door went forward about a quarter of a revolution – not enough to allow her to exit, but enough to close off her means of retreat – before it lurched to a halt and would not budge. She pushed at it, calmly at first, assuming it was merely jammed, but when it became apparent that it was stuck she threw all her weight against it, trying to shake it loose. The door rattled loudly but would not move and she kicked at it in frustration. Next she turned around and tried to push the it backwards, but, as she suspected, the tracking wouldn't run that way.

She tried to gather herself, to calm the pulse that was thundering in her temples, but instead panic set in and she moved about in a frenzy from side to side, trying to dislodge the door. It had no effect, the door shuddering and vibrating under her blows, but no more. At last she slid down to ground, her back against the glass, tears in her eyes and sweat streaming down her face. Her whole body began to tremble as she thought of what would happen if someone were to find her trapped here, or if no one did, if she were just left to starve and be set upon by the contaminated.

After some time Marta managed to calm herself and she began to think through how she could engineer an escape. Nothing came to mind and she had to fight down her panic again. The thin wedge of space she was trapped within seemed to be growing hotter by the moment, the sunlight beating through the panes of glass. Though she knew it was impossible she could not help imagining the stuffy air slowly draining from the place with each breath she took until she suffocated.

A flash of movement on the escalators above caught her eye and for a moment her heart leapt in excitement, only to be replaced by trepidation. No one would help her here. The Quarantine Patrol would not come for her even if she managed to contact them on the radio. She swallowed, telling herself that it had been nothing more than a change in the light, but the distinct sensation of being watched that crept across her neck told her otherwise. She leaned forward trying to parse the shadows above her, hope and fear wrestling in her mind. She thought she could make out something there, a vague form, but she couldn't be certain. No further movement came, though she waited expectantly.

"Fucking goddamn idiot," she said at last to herself.

The words seem to break a spell that had been cast. The shadows moved atop the escalator and she briefly made out the form of someone backing away quickly. She nearly called out, begging whoever it was to stay and help her. Before she could though there was a crash against the glass behind her and she whirled around to see a man, his face contorted into an awful grimace slamming himself against the immovable revolving door. She screamed and jumped to her feet, throwing herself against the door as hard as she could to no effect. The contaminated man yelled something unintelligible in response to her screams and redoubled his tortured efforts.

Unable to move the door more than a fraction the man next tried to squeeze himself into the crevice of space that led to the compartment adjacent to the one Marta was trapped in. Seeing this she moved as far as she could from him, her back pressed against the glass. She tried to breath through her mouth, as though the contamination were something like the hay fever she got in the spring which would send her into sneezing fits. She seemed unable to think, unable to move as the man struggled with the door, grunting and rasping, though she knew each additional moment she stayed here increased her chances of becoming contaminated.

At last the man succeeded in wedging himself within the door. As he did so he lurched forward, tripping on the door frame, and went head first into the next door pane, knocking himself senseless. Marta screamed again and darted to other side of the door which gave way and started to move again. Something the man had done in trying to get inside had managed to jar the door loose and she threw herself against it only to find that his prone body now blocked its path. Weeping with desperation she pushed again and again until at last she managed to work the door forward enough that she could slip out. She fled down the street, running without heed, the air feeling polluted in her lungs.

Jon spent a restless day alone, pacing a trail from the

window in the kitchen that overlooked the street below up to the terrace roof where he could see for blocks in any direction. Each time he would stop in the living room and turn on his radio, though he knew it was no use and he was just wasting the battery, to listen and see if Marta was trying to contact him or anyone. It was late in the afternoon now, the sun at its hottest on the terrace where he now kept a miserable vigil. If all had gone well Marta would have returned by now. A thousand scenarios, all with the same ending, played out in his mind. He had offered to go with her, but she had refused. It was her choice to get the prescription, she had said, so she should be the one to take the risk. He had tried to tell her that it didn't matter, he wanted to help her regardless of whether or not he agreed with her reason for going.

"Two of us will raise more questions than one," Marta had said and he could not find fault her reasoning there. The Quarantine Patrol were ruthless in their enforcement of proximity laws outside the space of people's homes. They had to be ruthless in everything they did, it had been the only thing to slow the spread of the contamination. If the cure was no better than the disease, was in fact the same as the disease, then that was the price to be paid.

Anyone who showed any sign of contamination was placed under quarantine before they could become more contagious and spread the disease farther. But quarantine no longer meant what it once had. As no traditional quarantine had proven effective in stopping the spread of the contamination, the Patrols had begun to execute people. The hours after someone showed signs of pollution were of course the hours when they were most contagious, and if there was no hope of survival, it was reasoned, better to end their misery now and hopefully spare some others the same fate.

There had been those who had rebelled against the Protocol, especially at first, but when all hope of a cure had in essence been abandoned most people had accepted it as a necessary horror in the midst of this nightmare. Those who could not, even in the face of certain extinction, had gone to live in the contaminated zones, crafting solitary existences while awaiting oblivion. He and Marta had been among the fortunate, if one could use that term for those who had survived, in that they had both managed to escape contamination, so leaving the Quarantine Zone had never been a question. They had both wanted to cling to what moments remained for as long as possible, each of them secretly harboring a dream that they would somehow survive this madness.

At last he could stand the wait no more and he retreated to the apartment next door to theirs to check on the beer he was brewing, the last of the batch he had bought during those frenzied days when the world had seemed as though it might well and truly collapse. It had been one of those purchases which later had seemed like the height of lunacy – why would he be making beer in the midst of the apocalypse – but which he had been extremely grateful for in the months that followed, for it had given him a task when all others had been taken from him. Even Marta, who had hated his home brewing when it had taken up the apartment in the days before the contagion had gotten involved in the process.

He had bottled the batch four days ago so there was really nothing to do now but wait for the yeast and sediment to settle. In spite of that he came into the abandoned apartment nearly every day just to look everything over, as though to assure himself that it was still there. This day his heart was not in it and he merely stared at the clouded bottles blankly. Finally he shook his head and left the room, returning to his apartment. He lay on the bed with his eyes closed, willing himself to empty his mind, all to no avail.

The apartment next door had belonged to a single man, probably close to their age, who they had seen rarely. Jon couldn't have even said what his name was, though Marta would know, would have talked to him. Jon had known him only to nod hello when they met in the hallways. He had known nothing about him beyond that. He had died in the early days of the contamination, when you could hardly walk the streets without coming across bodies. Most everything had still been working then, a majority of people still living and everyone seemingly contacting everyone they knew daily or hourly to ensure they were still alive, and yet he had been the one to find the man. He had been dead for several days and it was only the odor that had alerted them to the fact. A terrible smell, unfamiliar and yet he had known it instantly.

It had amazed him and appalled him at the time that someone could die without anyone noticing, without family or friends coming over to see whether or not he was alright. Now, he thought, we are all bound to face that eventuality, to die with no one who knows you left to mourn. The thought stayed with him as he watched the shadows move across the room and the light slowly die.

Marta waited all afternoon in an abandoned high rise on the edge of the Quarantine Zone to see if she was going to start showing symptoms. Shaking hands was what she had been told were the first to appear, then the wild mood swings and the inability to control one's emotions or expressions. For over an hour she had been convinced that she was already in the throes of contamination as she seemed to suffer each of these symptoms in succession, but she soon realized it was only shock from what had happened and fear of what was to come that she was experiencing. Once she had calmed herself and reasoned through what she needed to do she began to feel better. Then it was just a matter of waiting to see if the symptoms did in fact present themselves.

According to everything she had been told the first signs of contamination would appear within four hours of exposure. Not every exposure caused contamination of course, otherwise everyone still living would have been polluted multiple times over, it seemed as much a matter of luck as anything else. This was what she told herself as she waited, back against a wall, staring at her hands. There was still a chance she could return home. If not, if the worst happened, she had already promised herself that she would head back to the Quarantine Zone and turn herself over to the first patrol she encountered. That way, at least, Jon would know what had happened to her.

She waited through the rest of the morning and well into the afternoon, not moving from where she sat, hardly glancing away from the open doorway of office she had sequestered herself in. She had worked in a place like this once, one of hundreds squirreled away in her cubicle passing time to no end. It had only seemed all the more pointless in the aftermath of the unfolding crisis, processing invoices was not essential in this new world, if it had ever been. In spite of that she missed it, missed the routine, missed even the most mundane and annoying aspects that had left her exhausted and miserable at the end of the day.

When the light began to change in the office she knew the sun had begun its descent, but still she waited to be absolutely sure that she was well. What if she brought it back to Jon? What if it somehow passed by her and infected him? She knew that was impossible, at least as far as anyone knew. Transmission was only from the contaminated and she knew now that she was not infected. It had been five hours and the only symptom she had displayed was a panic that would not subside. That, she knew from hard experience, was only too normal. It had been her state of being for days during the first weeks of the contamination.

At last, knowing she couldn't delay any longer, she rose to her feet to return home, thinking about what she would tell Jon.

Marta would not meet his eyes when she spoke. She would look at him for the barest of seconds and then focus on whatever was just behind him, her eyes darting from wall to table to picture. She had returned home just before the curfew, the sun nearly gone from the sky, when her mere presence on the street would have meant an automatic engagement of the Quarantine Protocol. Her hair was disheveled and she stank of sweat, and while she tried to maintain an air of calm and ease with him, Jon could tell she was distraught by whatever had happened to her.

After spending the day and the evening alternating between worry and anger at her failure to return, the embers of both flames constantly stoked by his thoughts on the reason for her going and his inability to dissuade her from that task, Jon felt nothing but joy at the sight of her. Not relief that she was safe and well, but sheer and exuberant happiness that they were together still, after all that had transpired. He had tried to take her in his arms, wanting to feel her, to get the smell of her in his nostrils, but Marta had flinched at his approach and he had stayed back.

"How about I make us some supper?" he said.

"Yes. Yes."

He had started to prepare their meal, keeping up a steady patter of conversation as Marta had darted in and out of the kitchen, never resting anywhere for long, just as her eyes never steadied. Her responses were distant and monosyllabic, her thoughts obviously elsewhere, but he was patient. Whatever had happened she would tell him in her own time. Strangely, he felt no fear. Even as she was not herself, she was still herself, not the polluted thing he had seen so many others become.

After they had eaten the lentils and rice he had prepared and were each finishing their glasses of beer, he asked her, "What happened?"

The directness of his question seemed to startle her and

for the first time that evening she looked directly at him. "I got my prescription."

"And?" Jon said.

"And I left and there was someone who was contaminated outside. So I went a different way. To avoid him."

She seemed unable to say anymore, her eyes filling with tears. "But you didn't," Jon said to her. Marta shook her head. "You haven't noticed any symptoms?"

"No," she let loose a ragged sigh. "I waited. I waited until I was sure."

"How long?"

"Hours." She shrugged.

"Okay."

She began to cry, her face contorting as she tried to stop herself, but eventually she just gave in and let the tears flow, sobbing quietly. Jon resisted the urge to go comfort her, knowing she would only push him away. Instead he got up and took their plates to the sink and then sat down across from her again.

"I just," Marta started and then had to stop, the breath gone from her lungs. "I just can't stop seeing him. I can't stop thinking about it."

"You're just in shock. It will pass. We'll get through this."

"I'm so sorry."

"I know," Jon said. "There's no guarantees anywhere. Even if we just stayed here. I know that."

He poured them both another glass of beer and they both went out to the patio overlooking the empty courtyard and drank their beer watching the darkness come in. With the darkness came the bugs, mosquitoes and other flies and they were soon forced to retreat within. The world will be theirs soon, Jon thought, and then told himself that no, it would not. Somehow this would not be the end.

That thought in his mind he turned to Marta, unable to

stop himself from giving voice to the words that had been in his mind from the moment she had returned. He knew she would not agree, she had never before, though part of his mind told him that she had been so close to dying today that maybe she would this time. But the greater part of him knew, with certainty, how she would react, especially in her current overwhelmed state of mind.

"I think," he said, "We need to talk about whether you need to go out again. After today, it just seems like too much risk. You don't need the pill."

Her hands, Jon saw, were shaking violently, but her face was steady and calm. "I'm not going to talk about this with you. Not today."

"Why not today? Today of all days we should," he was unable to stop himself from saying the words, was compelled to, even as he knew she was right. He should be taking her in his arms, taking her to bed, never letting her go. "We need to. I don't want to lose you. Not over that."

It took a moment for Marta to master her emotions before she spoke. "You just said there were no guarantees. Even if we both stay here. There are none."

"Still. There's levels of risk."

"I agree. And I think this is worth it."

Jon walked away from her, stretching to relieve the tension that had coiled through his frame. He turned and looked back at Marta, his mouth working silently as he tried and then stopped himself from saying anything further.

"Jon," Marta said, an expression on her face that broke his heart to see. "I won't bring a child into this world. I don't care what the Protocol says. I won't do it."

"We always wanted a kid though," he said. He felt terrible saying it, knowing how much it hurt them both to hear it. Every time they had this conversation he would say it; part of him wanted it to hurt.

"We did," Marta said. "But not now. I won't do it now, not when there could be nothing left."

"There will be for sure if people like us don't have children."

"That's true. And maybe that's for the best, if this is the only kind of life left."

He wanted to argue with her further, and on another day he might have, but this day he gave in and fell silent. They stared at each other in awkward silence until Marta reached out with an open hand. He took it and she led him into their bedroom.

The next day passed in a silence marked by furtive glances and pained looks when the other was not watching. There were a few times when Marta was certain that Jon was going to start up their conversation from the night before again. He had always been insistent about the need for them to have a child, to ensure the humanity had a chance to continue, while she had always refused. She would not bring a child into a world where its parents would very likely be dead before it even had a chance to remember who they were or what they looked like. Any child would be unlikely to live anyway, given how susceptible children were to contamination. In the end it came down to the simple fact that Jon still believed in a future for them and for a child, while she was convinced these were humanity's last days.

There was no bridging that gap, and though they tried to talk around it, to sidestep the subject, it inevitably surfaced, especially after days like yesterday. There was no dealing with it, no resolution forthcoming, because it was tied directly to the basic facts of their existence. It could not be avoided. Instead they tried to avoid each other, Jon heading for the apartment where he was making his beer and Marta for the terrace upstairs and her garden. They ate separately and said little, each of them understanding that they needed time for the storm to pass.

Marta tried at supper that night. The Quarantine Patrol had made their weekly supply drop off that afternoon and included in it were a couple of thin and gristly looking steaks. Once the power was turned on for the evening she put them in a pot with a can of mushroom soup and some onion, garlic and a pepper and let it simmer for an hour until the meat was tender. There were noodles to go with it and she picked some tomatoes and a cucumber from the terrace garden. She poured out some beer for each of them and then found Jon in one of the other abandoned apartments reading an old magazine.

Jon sat with her and ate the meal, but he would not speak, though she tried to engage him, asking him how his last batch of beer was coming and how he planned to go about making some more. Normally their conversation was effortless, complemented with easy silences. They could fill the hours and yet talk of nothing more than the garden, his beer, or what they'd heard on the latest Quarantine Patrol radio broadcast. Jon was always joking with her, even after the worst of their fights he would try to get her to laugh, to lighten the mood and distract them both from what was going on. If anything he was the one who needed conversation, even if it was meaningless, serving only to fill the silence.

Which was what made it so strange that he would not say anything to her at supper. Even in their worst moments they would still fight their way through the awkwardness and resentment and find something to say. But not that night and she could not fathom why, for as raw and fundamental as their argument the night before had been, it was by no means the worst between them. If anything he had held back, reluctant to push her, given the emotional state she had been in. So for him today to still be mired in those thoughts gave her pause.

She watched Jon closely the rest of the night. He joined her on the patio to watch the sunset as they did every night, neither of them unable to shake free of the ingrained habits of their day. They both craved that normalcy in the face of the abnormality of the entire world around them.

Marta tried the opposite tact to the one she had employed at dinner, saying nothing at all, and seeing if that would draw him out. But he was silent, looking off into the sky at the clouds turned red and purple in the sun.

When the insects chased them both inside she turned on the radio to listen to the evening Protocol broadcast. It was the usual litany of ominous developments hidden behind a facade of hopeful statements about ongoing promising research that was certain to lead to a cure. The general thrust was always the same. The system continued towards complete breakdown, with fewer and fewer people left to manage it. Normally Jon would have spent the broadcast making barbed barbed comments, but he did not appear to listen to anything that was said.

When the power went out for the night he helped her light the candles. Their hands brushed against each other as they exchanged matches, but his face showed no expression at all. She read for a bit before going to bed and he sat across from her, seeming to not even look at her, though she tried to catch his eye more than once. He did not avoid her gaze, he seemed oblivious to it. She tried smiling at him once, trying to draw some reaction out of him, but none came. He sat across from her in the deeply shadowed room, his face blank, his eyes unreadable.

Marta went to bed, unable to take anymore, and Jon joined her, turning his back to her in the bed without even offering a kiss goodnight. After a few minutes she heard his breathing deepen. It was all so unlike him. The night before, after the throes of their argument he had been unable to sleep. That had always been his way. Instead it was she who could not sleep, who lay awake unable to stop the thoughts that worried at her mind. What was the matter with Jon? But she knew it could only be one thing.

Jon let his breathing go steady as though he were asleep and waited for Marta's to do the same. It was some time, perhaps two hours, before she finally drifted off. When he was certain that she was asleep he slipped out of bed and left the room, going to sit alone in the living room. He could still hear Marta's breathing there, the building and the city around them so quiet now with the power gone and the streets outside empty but for the odd Quarantine Patrol car. He listened to her breathing carefully, trying to see if he could notice any difference from before, but there was none.

The other changes were more apparent. They could, he knew, just be a consequence of the fright she had had with the contaminated man the day before. It could be nothing, and yet, he knew from hard experience, having seen it before with his father and Marta's sister, that these small, seemingly insignificant, differences in personality were the result of something larger. Before they would have passed without comment, a bad day or poor night's sleep, but now they would manifest themselves into something that would become only too apparent soon enough. In the meantime he had to decide what to do.

He went over again what had happened since she had been exposed to reassure himself that his judgment was correct. There were the unaccounted hours, which could be explained by her fear that she had been contaminated, or they could mean something more. Then there was the way she had acted after she had returned, skittish and looking as though she might take flight at any moment. During their argument she had acted as she normally would have, it had reassured him oddly enough. But the next day the strange behaviors had continued to mount until he could not ignore them.

She had seemed to want to avoid him during the morning so he had let her be. Her hands, he had noticed, still shook sometimes, the slightest of tremors. Perhaps she had not recovered from the shock yet, he told himself. It had put him on his guard and he had been careful not to react to anything she did. At supper she had tried multiple times to talk to him, almost desperately he thought, as though the quiet frightened her. Then after, as they had listened to the broadcast, she had kept staring at him wildly.

And tonight she had not been able to fall asleep. Normally she drifted off without effort, much to his frustration, for it would often take him an hour or more. It could be nothing, he told himself. No one thing could be taken as evidence that she had been contaminated. She had not shown any of the more serious symptoms yet. Those would come soon enough, though, and what would he do then?

The next morning when Marta awoke Jon was not in bed beside her. She could hear him in the kitchen making breakfast. For a moment she thought she would cry, but she mastered the upsurge of emotions before they could overwhelm her and got out of bed to join him. They ate in silence, sharing wary smiles as they watched each other. She still felt exhausted, as though she had not slept at all through the night. Jon looked the same, she thought, heavy bags under his eyes and a sluggishness about him.

Every movement he made she searched for the hidden signs of his contamination that he would display unconsciously. It was apparent in everything. He was withdrawn and distant still, keeping himself at a remove from her at all times. And watching her, that she noticed as well. Does he know, she wondered? In some ways she didn't want to look at him anymore, it was all too heartbreaking, and yet she could not look away. These might very well be his last hours, their last moments together. Already he was not the man she knew, he was something different. Soon it would be worse, much worse. Did she want to be witness to that?

After breakfast she went up to the garden to water the plants and then stayed there on the terrace trying to decide what to do. She knew what she had to do, there was no doubt there. It was just a matter of doing so. She stayed, checking all the plants again and fingering the soil, unable to bring herself leave yet.

The door to the terrace opened behind her and Jon came out, smiling uneasily at her. She nodded and smiled in return, trying to put a brave face on, though she felt her hand shaking. He stood and watched her as she worked, while she tried to ignore his presence. She had the distinct feeling, how she could not say, that he was trying to find the words to tell her something, but he never spoke. At last she finished all the busywork she could manage and she led them both back downstairs to their apartment, their every step weighted, it seemed to her, with the eventuality of what was to come.

The Quarantine Patrol was waiting for them. There were four of them, all in bio-hazard suits, three with hands on their guns. The fourth, who was standing in front of the others, motioned gently with one hand.

"Marta Gilovic, you have been reported for Quarantine Protocol."

"What?" she said in disbelief, looking at Jon.

"Please don't make this more difficult, Marta," he said, putting his hands on her shoulders as though to calm her.

She shrugged him off and looked at the Patrolmen. "This is insane. He's the one who's been contaminated. He's the one showing symptoms."

The Patrolmen looked from person to person, as though at a glance they might determine who was telling the truth.

"Marta," Jon said again, in the tone one would use when speaking to a child, "You've not been yourself since you were exposed. The tremor in your hand. And last night at dinner."

"I was in shock. And you were acting differently. Withdrawn. Your eyes look strange. They're not the way they normally are."

Jon took a step away from her, a look of horror growing on his face. "I am not contaminated."

The nearest Patrolman stepped forward so that he stood in between both of them. "When did you have contact with the contaminated?"

"Two days ago," Marta said slowly.

"Where were you?"

"I was downtown."

"Outside the Quarantine Zone."

"Yes," Marta said, her face going flush as her hand started to tremble again. "I needed to refill my prescription."

"She does not want a child," Jon said by way of explanation.

"I waited five hours, to make sure that I was showing no symptoms before I came home. I felt fine. I feel fine. Then yesterday he started to act differently. He wouldn't talk to me, he was distant and withdrawn. Unemotional. Very unlike him. And his eyes, as I said."

"My eyes are the same as they've always been," Jon said. He pointed at Marta, "She was not the same when she came home. She was not the same yesterday. She may say there were no symptoms, but I see symptoms. What other explanation is there?"

"For god's sake Jon, I was in shock."

The Patrolman raised his hands again and they both stopped, looking at each other wide-eyed as they realized they had been shouting. Marta raised a hand to her mouth. The Patrolman stepped away from them, motioning to the others who stepped forward, guns now drawn from their holsters.

"Permission to enact Quarantine Protocol," he said into the radio sewn into his suit.

There was a pause as they waited for a response that seemed to stretch on into infinity, Marta and Jon staring at each other as though they did not recognize themselves. A muffled, static-ridden voice sounded in each suit.

"Confirmed."

THE HORNS

1

In the year 1625 of Our Lord, in Cartagena, that magnificent and redoubtable coastal fort in the Viceroyalty of Peru, Don Santiago Alvarez de Armias awoke one day to discover horns upon his head. They were long and narrow, curving slightly upward from his forehead, not unlike an goat's. Or a demon's, as his servants and slaves whispered to each other upon seeing it. Most of them fled his house in the days that followed, for they had a premonition of the trials that awaited him.

These began, if there is such a thing as beginnings and endings, the day prior, when Don Santiago met some acquaintances on the streets beyond the Plaza de los Coches, where he had come from looking at some slaves on offer at the market. The full heat of the day was upon them and they elected to retire to a nearby tavern to take some sustenance there. One of the men, a notorious cocksman named Armando Gonzago, told the other men a salacious tale of his latest conquest, who he had been with that very morning while Don Santiago was at the slave market. So tempestuous was their lovemaking, Armando claimed, that they broke the baluster on the bed. All three men laughed at the thought of the poor cuckold who would return home to a broken bed and his wife's poor excuses. Which he would no doubt believe, for Armando noted he had been so oblivious to this point that he did not suspect anything was amiss.

The three men finished their oruja and said their goodbyes. Don Santiago went about the rest of his day, giving little thought to Armando's tale. It was evening by the time he returned home. As he let one of his servants wash his face with a damp towel, his wife called out to him that he would need to see to the repair of their marriage bed, whose baluster had somehow become broken.

Don Santiago went still at her words. "How did it become broken?" he said.

"I only noticed it this afternoon," she said, as though that were an explanation.

As if in a dream, Don Santiago recalled other instances of her evasions from his questions, other times when she had offered no explanation for strange incidents and absences. An incredible anger began to build inside him. His whole body seemed to tremble, as though assailed by a tempest. Words failed him.

When he recovered himself somewhat he strode into the bedroom to investigate and saw that, indeed, the baluster had been snapped in half. He strove to peer through the dim mists of his memory to that very morning when he had risen from bed. How had the baluster appeared then? Solid and whole, just as the frame itself. Now here it lay upon the floor, as broken as his trust in everything his wife told him.

Don Santiago called her into the room, demanding that she explain herself.

"I don't know. It was fine this morning, but when I came in this afternoon I found it so. Perhaps," and here she lowered her voice, so that only he could hear, "the servants were about where they should not have been."

Don Santiago stared at her, numb and cold, all emotion having fled. He turned to look at the mestizo boy who attended him when he was at home, but the boy would not meet his gaze. A terrible shudder overcame him, as though a spirit had passed across his grave. He bent down to seize the offending piece of wood and turned back to his wife, who studied him with a bemused expression on her face.

His rage returned to him, overwhelming, coursing through his veins like a torrential river. He struck his wife with what remained of the baluster, knocking her stunned to the floor. A trickle of blood ran from her head down between her eyes. Blow after blow he rained down upon her, until she lay upon the floor in an ever-growing pool of blood.

Servants were screaming, footsteps sounding throughout the rest of the house. Don Santiago could not hear them over the thunder of the pulse in his ears. His head ached and he felt exhilarated beyond belief. He looked from his wife to the mestizo boy who remained standing, his lips quivering wordlessly, too afraid to move lest he draw his master's ire.

The baluster was still in his hand and he tossed it to the floor beside his wife, gesturing to the boy. He would not come, still staring in mute horror.

"Here boy," Don Santiago said, "listen. Go summon the Alcalde quick."

The servant would still not move and Don Santiago had to drag him from the room to send him on his way. When the boy was on gone, he turned back into the bedroom trying to gather what remained of his thoughts. The Alcalde would need clear evidence that his had been a righteous fury, justified by his wife making him a fool and a cuckold. As he pondered this, he looked upon the broken form of his wife and saw her mouth opening and closing oddly, as though she had lost all command of it. Her body writhed on the floor, as if she were in the throes of an awful ecstasy.

One of the other servants tried to come tend to her, but Don Santiago chased her away with the baluster, forbidding anyone else coming near in a voice that sounded tinged with madness. He sealed the door to their chambers and crouched beside his wife. As he stared into her dying eyes, he tried to think of something to say, a fitting closure to their lives together and her utter betrayal of his honor. But his wife surprised him by speaking before he could.

"I curse you, Don Santiago Alvarez de Armias, a feckless lover and inattentive husband, for all time. You will never rest easy again."

With those words she died, before Don Santiago could summon a response. He remained crouched at her side, her curse reverberating in his ears. Though she had perished, he could have sworn he felt her hand upon his head and he leapt back from her in horror, falling to the floor at the edge of the bed. It was in this position that the Alcalde discovered him.

After, as he prepared for bed, Don Santiago would think that the strange moment—the seeming possession of his wife by an enraged spirit—had been fortuitous in the end. The Alcalde had arrived and witnessed the whole bizarre scene, with Don Santiago's expression one of fear and madness. It was all of a piece with his claim, that he had been seized by an inordinate anger, a rage beyond all meaning, at his realization his wife had so utterly betrayed him.

He had answered the Alcalde's questions, the notary scrawling his answers, as someone saw to the removal of the body. His servants cleaned the room as best they could and, when the Alcalde was done with his interview, everyone left him alone in the bedroom. Don Santiago stared at the bloodstained floor and his bloody clothes for a time, before snuffing out the candles and going to bed. The darkness seemed to swim around him, alive and sinister, before he at last drifted off to sleep

2

His dreams that night were turbulent. He started awake several times, convinced that he was not alone, that someone or something was in the room with him. After a time the feeling left him and he returned to sleep. When he awoke to the light of morning he had no memory of the dreams, only of those brief moments of wakefulness when his mind had been empty of all but an overwhelming fear at the unseen presence nearing him. His body was aching, his head particularly, and he felt exhausted as though he had not slept at all.

As he rose from bed his head seemed heavy and sluggish, almost difficult to lift. One of his servants entered his room. When Don Santiago turned to greet her, she fled in horror. He watched her go, a terrible realization settling upon him. He reached up to touch his forehead and could feel them protruding. Their length was terrifying. How had they grown so in the space of one night? Shuddering, he went to find a looking glass to see for himself.

His wife had one sitting atop the bureau of her dresser, which he was now afraid to touch. It took him some time to lift it up and more time still before he could actually bring himself to look. He could see the blood drain from his face, his hands and feet going numb. Only when he was certain that he was not going to faint, did he study the horns closely. There was one above each of his eyes near the top of his forehead where his hair began, thrusting upward in parallel. They were not as long as he had thought, resembling those of a goat, though there were the beginnings of a curve to them, suggesting they would continue to grow. The thought was terrifying.

As he set down the mirror, he became aware of the murmur from the rest of household. The girl had told them what she had seen, and now they were debating what to do, if they should flee before the demon that possessed him took hold of them as well. He stepped out of the room, cursing them all as superstitious Indians and pointed at one of the men, Tadeo.

"You," he said. "Bring a saw and come to me."

When Tadeo had retrieved a saw and returned to the house, Don Santiago bade him to cut the horns from his head.

The pain was indescribable. He lost consciousness twice, but each time he awoke and insisted that Tadeo continue with his work. The servant appeared as though he wanted to refuse, and there were cries of horror from the others who watched, but Don Santiago insisted. There was a mad gleam to his eyes, which even he could sense, and perhaps it was that which compelled Tadeo to see the job done.

Whatever it was, the task was soon complete. Only stubs remained, just visible above his hair. Don Santiago ordered the horns burnt and swore all his servants to secrecy on the matter. The terror in their eyes convinced him they would do so. He was a fearful sight, blood still seeping from the stubs into his hair and down his face and clothes, his eyes still in a wild frenzy from the pain. He was left weak by the loss of so much blood and was forced to retire again to his broken bed in order to recover his strength.

When he awoke late in the day, he saw that he should not have trusted his servants, for word had spread far and wide and a crowd had gathered outside the house, awaiting his emergence. Don Santiago flew into a rage at the sight of so many people gathered simply to gawk at his suffering. He flung chamber pots and cups and whatever else was at hand at the servants who were close by, cursing and calling them all manner of foul names.

When he had thrown all that he could put hand to, he retrieved his sword, intending to draw blood from all of them, until someone confessed to their misdeed. The servants and slaves did not allow him the opportunity. Those who had remained in the house through his tirade fled as soon as he drew his sword, running into the street and telling those assembled that their master Don Santiago was possessed by magic or a demon.

The resulting murmurs of consternation reached Don Santiago's ears, his rage evaporating in an instant, replaced by shame at what he had done. He stepped out of his house, still carrying his sword, his face still streaked with blood, an abject apology on his lips. Those gathered reacted in horror to the sight of him. There were screams and shouts as people fled. A woman fainted in terror and was trampled in the resulting stampede. Don Santiago slunk back inside, bolting the door behind him, swearing that he would not emerge until his head had healed and the stumps had withered away.

There was little food in the house and no one to cook it, but Don Santiago had no appetite anyway. He simply returned to bed and tried to sleep away his misery. It was not until evening came that he thought of his young son and went to see if the boy was still about. There was no one in the house and Don Santiago was left both enraged and relieved. One of the servants must have taken him, he decided, which was far beyond their call. But hopefully they knew enough to take the child to his mother's parents, who resided in Cartagena. Better that he remain there for the time being, than to be forced to witness his father in such a state.

Don Santiago awoke the next morning feeling refreshed and invigorated. His head still ached and felt disjointed, he assumed from his wounds, until he saw his visage in the looking glass. When he did, he let out a terrible cry that resounded across the neighborhood. The horns had regrown during the night and were now as long and heavy as they had been the day before. It seemed this was his fate.

He refused to leave the house, suffering from a melancholy that suffused his entire flesh. No hope remained and he contemplated all manner of terrible deeds to relieve himself of this misery. His conscience and his faith in Our Lord stayed his hand, but only barely.

As the day went on his depression began to abate somewhat and he started to think on ways that he might escape the curse his wife had bequeathed him. It seemed obvious that some magic or demon was involved and mere faith in the savior would not be enough to save him. He would need the assistance of someone versed in counteracting maleficios, or perhaps conducting an exorcism to remove the demonic power of the horns. That was a last resort though, for it seemed preferable not to involve the Church, if at all possible. There was very real chance they would turn him over for investigation by the Inquisition.

He was not to escape that fate either, for as he was plotting how he would contact someone skilled in the arts of magic and necromancy, one Doctor Don Ezequiel de Cabrera y Ruis, Inquisitor of the Holy Inquisition knocked upon his door. A notary stood behind him, ready to transcribe the interview. Though his heart was quailing, Don Santiago allowed the Inquisitor entry to his home and sat down to answer his questions.

"When did the protuberances first make themselves

apparent?" Don Ezequiel said, in a calm and measured voice, looking upon Don Santiago as though he was referring to a boil or infection.

Don Santiago told him everything, beginning with his wife's infidelity and his murder of her, leaving nothing out. There was no point in trying to hide from the Inquisitor, he would have it out of him anyway, by one means or another.

"I have spoken with the Alcalde on the matter of your wife's death," Don Ezequiel said. "A most understanding man. He has agreed to suspend the trial for the moment, to allow me time to determine the provenance of these things."

"I have told you their provenance," Don Santiago said, his voice breaking with despair.

"Hmm," Don Ezequiel said, pursing his lips. "It is an unlikely story, isn't it? I have heard many tales of witchcraft and maleficio in my day. Possession by demon and all the rest. And in the end, in most cases, it is mere superstition that drives these things. The uneducated, the more easily swayed among us, can be persuaded that such things exist, when in point of fact they do not."

Don Santiago was left dumbfounded. The Inquisitor seemed unpersuaded by the evidence that lay before his very eyes. "Do you not see the horns atop my head?"

"One cannot fail to notice," Don Ezequiel said mildly. "Their appearance so soon after the death of your wife is rather convenient, I would note. As are the fits of madness your servants and neighbors speak of you suffering since that night."

"How do you suppose these came to be here?" Don Santiago said, spitting the words at the Inquisitor.

He raised a careful eyebrow. "There are any number of tricks charlatans might attempt to persuade the gullible. Anyone who has spent an evening at the theater knows the costumes and masks one can assume. I see nothing here that convinces me this is anything other than that."

Though he knew it was lunacy itself to confront an Inquisitor, Don Santiago could contain himself no longer and flew into a rage. He cursed the man, cursed his wife for what she had done, slamming his fist upon the table. "I cut them off," he said pointing at the horns. "And yet they have returned. I shall never be free of them."

"So you say," Don Ezequiel said, not having reacted to anything Don Santiago had said, except to glance at the notary to confirm he was recording it all.

He left shortly thereafter, promising Don Santiago that they would speak again soon. The words echoed in his ears long after the Inquisitor was gone and he was left alone in his house. The silence seemed to answer back with a question that would haunt him in the coming days: What was to become of him?

3

That evening hunger drove him from his home. He dressed himself in a cloak, as though he were a monk, drawing the cowl over his head in an attempt to hide his monstrous new appendages. He still felt self-conscious as he made his way along the streets, being careful to keep to the shadows lest someone recognize him. Instead of going to the usual taverns or homes where he would formerly have spent his evenings, he stayed to the poorer parts of town, where he was unlikely to encounter anyone he knew.

For the most part he was ignored, even when he kept his cowl up on his head as he sat at a tavern and had a drink and meal. When he was finished he asked the proprietor, a mestizo looking man of indeterminate age, if he knew of someone who could counteract maleficios. The proprietor peered closely at him for the first time, as if to ascertain what his intentions were, and told him a single name, "Sister Juanita."

The man declined to say anything more on the matter and it was some time before Don Santiago could find anyone who would tell him anything about the mysterious Sister Juanita. Finally a trull, who would not meet his gaze, even in the darkness of the street, told him he could find her near the Augustine Convent of Nuestra Señora de la Candelaria. Don Santiago knew the place well, for the convent sat on a hill overlooking Cartagena itself, having been inaugurated twenty years earlier. Though it was over an hour's walk away, along a treacherous path up the hillside, made all the more so because it was night, he determined to go. The burden of the horns upon his head was simply too much to bear for a moment longer and he needed to find out if there was any chance he could be free of them.

It took much longer than an hour for him to summit the hill, for he lost his way on the several paths that crossed along it due to the darkness. By the time he reached the top he could see the beginnings of the sunrise upon the horizon and the bells of the convent were sounding, calling the nuns to morning prayers. He was weak with thirst and hunger from his journey and desperately wanted to throw himself upon the door of the convent to beg for whatever sustenance they might provide, but his shame at his awful appearance made him turn aside.

Instead, he wandered about the vast hillside behind the convent, asking the few people who were awake at such an hour where he might find Sister Juanita. Most would not even acknowledge his presence, one caught a glimpse of the horns hidden beneath his cowl and immediately fled. With no guidance, he chose his path at random and ended up on a long and winding trail that seemed as though it must surely lead off the hill and back to the city itself.

Somehow it did not, for when he had passed out of a small forest that lay behind the convent, he emerged to find himself overlooking the city from nearly the same vantage point as the monastery. Yet the convent buildings were nowhere to be seen. He had also been walking for nearly an hour, and though the trail had wandered some, and he had taken a few wrong turns into dead ends, it still did not explain how he had spent so much time to arrive at a spot that, by all appearances, was so near where he had begun.

Don Santiago was still contemplating this apparent magic when a woman's voice called out to him. He whirled around and saw a small hut with smoke coming from its chimney, just visible through the tangle of trees behind him. Somehow he had missed it when he passed through the forest the first time. Looking at it now, he couldn't imagine how he had failed to notice it, but he assumed it was simply another trick of the landscape.

"I understand you are looking for me," the woman said again.

She had materialized near him, presumably emerging from the trees surrounding the house. Don Santiago had not heard her approach and was startled to find her so near. By appearance and her dress, he guessed she was a mestizo, though it was hard to say precisely. Her face was unlined, but her hair was white and he could not have put a number to her age. She gazed at him with eyes so dark they seemed black pools, beckoning him forward into their depths.

It was some time before he could find the words to speak. "You are Sister Juanita?"

"And you are Don Santiago Alvarez de Armias, wearer of the horns."

Her words chilled him. How had she known his name?

He tried to calm himself by saying that his cursed appendages were obvious, even with the cowl covering his head. The story of what had befallen him had, no doubt, spread far and wide. It was still shocking to realize it had gone beyond the walls of Cartagena, but he had to realize that even should he succeed in having the horns removed, he would still be haunted by innuendo and tales for the rest of his days.

Despair choked at him as he tried to formulate his words. "I would like…I was told I should speak to you about the removal of maleficios."

"Come with me," Sister Juanita said, waving for him to follow.

She led him on a path he had not seen, branching from the main one he had followed, through the trees to the hut. It was a squat building, with a low doorway he had to crouch to pass through. Within there was hardly any room to move at all. There were herbs and flowers hanging from the straw roof to dry, giving the hut a glorious earthy smell. The walls were lined with shelves, littered with jars filled with elixirs and concoctions and things Don Santiago hesitated to name.

The dirt floor too was populated with jars and other containers, so that it was difficult to maneuver, though Sister Juanita seemed to have no issue, stepping around various obstructions and gesturing for him to sit at the table. It was covered with an endless array of yet more herbs and elixirs, as well as various tools and implements, and a chicken waiting to be plucked. There was only one chair, so Don Santiago took it, sitting gingerly on its edge while he studied the hut and its owner.

She was busy by the fire, setting a pot over it to boil, humming tunelessly to herself. From time to time she pulled some herbs from the ceiling, or retrieved something from one of her many containers, to stir into whatever concoction she was making. Its smell was intoxicating and Don Santiago's hunger returned to him, setting his head aching. She was so oblivious to him as she made her preparations that he began to wonder if she had forgotten he was there at all. He tried to think of something to say that would alert her to his presence, but words failed him, and in the end he simply pulled back his cowl so that his horns were exposed.

"Now there we are," she said, as though he had given her a signal to begin. She found a bowl from the clutter on the table and filled it with steaming broth from the pot on the fire and handed it to him. "Drink up, you will need it."

Don Santiago accepted it from her, eyeing it doubtfully.

"What is it?"

"A restorative. Your broth is weak, yes? This will return the marrow to your bones."

Don Santiago flushed with anger, instinctively ducking his head as though preparing to ram her with his horns. "There is marrow to my bones. I'll draw swords with the man who says otherwise."

Sister Juanita chuckled to herself, shaking her head. "The horns on your head say otherwise. No marrow there. Your wife, God rest her soul, went searching for another starling to fill her nest."

"I did not come here to be mocked by the likes of you chunchu," Don Santiago said, rising so quickly from the table his horns became tangled in some of herbs hanging above him.

"No, you came seeking my help. Well, drink. Drink. I will help you soon enough."

Don Santiago returned to his seat, eyeing Sister Juanita with hostility. But he picked up the bowl and took a tentative sip as she had requested. The broth was clear but strong tasting and savory. The instant it touched his tongue he hungered for more and in no time he had drunk the bowl away.

"Good, good," Sister Juanita said. "Now, tell me, what can I do for you?"

Don Santiago stared at her in disbelief. "I would like these removed, and the curse that was laid upon me lifted. What else would I possible want?"

Sister Juanita shook her head. "That, I am afraid, cannot be done."

"I thought you could remove maleficios?"

"Yes, yes." Sister Juanita shuffled away to refill his bowl with her savory broth. Don Santiago drank it hungrily. "But this is no maleficio. This is what you are made visible."

"This is not what I am," Don Santiago cried out, throwing his bowl aside. "My wife gave me the horns to wear. Not I."

"You have always worn them. You just were not aware."

"Are you saying I have been cuckolded by life? Such a thing is not possible. It is my wife who has cuckolded me. She has made me wear the horns."

Sister Juanita gave him a sad smile. "I cannot say what your wife did or did not. It matters little. The horns have nothing to do with her, you understand. They were there, they have always been there. Now you know, now you know."

Don Santiago reacted with fury to her words, rising up and again plunging his horns into the mass of herbs and flowers hanging above him. He tossed his head aside, trying to free it from these unwelcome encumbrances, as he grappled for the sword, snarling at Sister Juanita.

"Vile chunchu. I should have known not to waste my time with you. I'll brand you with my sword, damnable witch."

Clouds swarmed across his vision as he tried to bring his sword up to strike Sister Juanita down. The hut he was in seemed to evaporate, dissipating like fog in sunshine, and he could no longer see the old woman. The taste of the broth was on his lips and he shouted, "You have poisoned me."

There was no response and the light began to swirl around his eyes, darkness following behind.

4

Don Santiago awoke some time later on a bed of damp moss in the midst of some trees. His head was groggy and he worried that he might vomit. The sun was near to setting and the shadows surrounding him were long. There was no sign of the woman or her hut, but he could still taste the broth in his mouth. He felt at his side for his sword but it was not there and a quick glance around his immediate vicinity did not reveal its presence.

It had to be somewhere, he told himself, and got to his feet unsteadily. He sought out the path he had taken to arrive at Sister Juanita's, reasoning that he must have stumbled into the trees while trying to escape from her before he succumbed utterly to her potion. Try as he might, he could find no sign of the trail he had taken, no sign of any habitations. The forest around him was thick with luxurious foliage and underbrush, and he had to fight his way through. His face and hands were soon marked with scratches and his clothing thick with burs. His horns gave him particular problems, seeming to catch themselves on every vine and stray branch.

How, in the name of God, had he come to be here? The question made him shudder in horror and rage.

For the hours of daylight that still remained, Don Santiago struggled through the forest, trying in vain to find the path—any path—that would lead him out. Again and again, he told himself that it was impossible for the forest to be so large. It would take an hour, two at most, to traverse the longest part of the hill, and yet he had been here for what now felt like days. He could see no sign of a trail, no glimpse of the convent, no sign of any habitation at all. It was impossible, all impossible—his horns, Sister Juanita, his missing sword, this hill—his mind refused to bend to this reality.

He slept that night in the forest and the next day, when he awoke, he saw the trail, only a few feet away from where he had rested and went to it. From there he rushed back to where he was certain Sister Juanita's house was, only to find that he emerged from the forest near the convent. A young Indian boy gawked at the sight of him.

Desperate now, Don Santiago reversed course along the trail, marking the trees as he went, so that he could be certain he was not being led astray by any of Sister Juanita's magics. It did not take him long to arrive at the forest's edge on the other side of the hill, overlooking a tremendous valley. Convinced that he must somehow have missed a branch or a byway in the path that had led him to the old woman's hut, he retraced his steps, following the marked trees, and arrived where he had begun.

It was as mystifying as the horns upon his head and there was no explanation for it. Yet Don Santiago persisted. He spent the day searching the entire forest, roaming through it as best he could. He did so without difficulty, always finding the path or the forest's limits with ease. There was no sign of Sister Juanita, her hut, or his sword.

At last he gave up and returned home. There he decided there was little point in his remaining in Cartagena. The Inquisitor would be bringing his case against him soon. He would be lucky to escape punishment, and even if he did, what life was left to him? He was a figure of mockery throughout the city: his wife had betrayed him and his own servants and slaves had abandoned him. His business ventures would fail, for who would trust a man whose honor was so visibly stained?

He left at nightfall, going out to the docks where he hired a fisherman—the only one of a group of men, sharing a bottle of aguardiente around a fire, willing to give him passage—to take him across to a small island just beyond the city's harbor. The island was uninhabited, but for the birds that nested on the cliffs along its southern shore. At its center was a small forest, which was where Don Santiago made his home, collecting rainwater to drink and fishing and killing birds for something to eat. There were fruit trees as well—coconuts and mangoes, among others—in amongst the trees, so he lived well.

In later times, the island became known as the Horns. Some sailors said it was because of the way its southern edge jutted out, with two narrow peninsulas pointing in the direction of Cartagena. Others knew the tale of Don Santiago Alvarez de Armias, and they always insisted upon stopping at the island to make an offering to his spirit, which, it was said, still resided there.

When, after nearly a century had passed, a ship was wrecked nearby and the sailors forced to swim to the island, they discovered a small herd of wild goats had made their home at the island's center. It was some days before another ship passed near enough for them to be rescued and so the sailors captured the goats and had a feast as they waited.

THE MOUTH OF THE UNDERWORLD

"Help me. I am here. Help me. I am trapped."

The words, carried on the wind, from somewhere within the mountain, were so faint I could barely make them out. I leaned forward, straining to see if there was any more to be heard, but only the sharp whistle of the wind on stone and the stirring of the trees behind me reached my ears. I stayed rooted where I was for five minutes or more, my sweat cooling on my back, but the voice did not return. I stood on the threshold of the Mouth of the Underworld, peering uneasily into the darkness that lay beyond the narrow ingress, knowing that I had to step within that void, but fearing to cross into that unknown realm.

My father had forbidden me to enter this place, and it was not in me to disobey him.

"Only the past lies there," he had said. "We have forgotten the entrance for a reason."

I could have argued that the past was who we were, that we had to face it and exorcise those demons if we were to ever be free of the Ven and their rule. But I had not, for there were many in Huispar who still believed in demons, in the terrible gods of the deep our ancestors had once worshipped. They believed the old laws still applied and that no Hautlyrun should enter the caves, for they were the path to the underworld, where the living had no place. That I knew differently did not matter, the cataman's son had to obey the ancient laws.

The breeze coming from the mouth of the cave died and silence descended in the surrounding cloud forest, as though the whole world was hushed, awaiting my decision. I had imagined the words, I told myself, imagined the voice, my own disquiet playing tricks on my mind.

But, even if that were true, it did not matter. Jasryl was still down there somewhere below. He had been gone for the better part of two days and there was nowhere else he could be. I had to go after him, because no one else would dare. More than that, he was the truest friend I had in this world. If I left him to die I would never be able to forgive myself, no matter that it went against my father's word and my own nature.

The decision made, I felt the weight lift from my shoulders. I slid through the narrow gap, the jagged edges of the stone almost touching my arms, giving me the distinct sensation of teeth closing in for a bite. I tried to ignore the feeling, though it was difficult, telling myself it was just the stories I had heard as a child coming to life in my head.

Three days before I had crossed this same threshold with Jasryl. That had been a different occasion, both of us filled with awe and excitement. Now every harbinger seemed to point toward doom.

I knelt in the opening of the cave where there was still enough light that I could see and fought with the lantern I had brought, trying to get it to stay lit. The wind was very strong, gusting at times, almost sweet smelling, alive with the earth itself. As I crouched over the lantern, trying to spark the oil, the words came on the wind again, more distinct this time, the voice clearly recognizable.

"Help me. I am here. Help me. I am trapped."

The entrance to the cave had been lost for several lifetimes, until Jasryl and I found it while exploring in the cloud forest in the mountains that surrounded Huispar. The caves that ran through the mountains had long been the source of tales among our people, involving the end of the beginning of the world, and gods and demons and such. Now they were little more than stories used to frighten children to bed.

The Mouth of the Underworld, it was called. Any who passed through it were eaten and became lost souls. It was some unfortunates emerged years or decades later, their bodies twisted and gnarled, their feet pointing backwards and their eyes gone blind.

Such tales carried a great deal less weight after the Ven brought the railroad through the mountains to Huispar and, with it, entry into Niedellun. Jasryl and I were the first generation of Hautlyren to grow up with no memory of a time before the railroad, and we embraced this new era with open arms, while our parents talked of the old ways and shook their heads sadly. Before the railroad Huispar had been isolated, little more than a village, places like Yurital as fabulous as any tale told of the Mouth to the Underworld. Now it was Yurital and the rest of Niedellun that were the eaters of souls, for many, like my older brother, had gotten aboard the train never to return.

We had no lanterns with us that first day, so we could only descend a short way past the narrow fissure that provided the entrance, before the darkness became too great. We stood for a time in the cave's mouth, peering at the impenetrable dark that lay beyond. Gusts of wind struck our faces, coming from far below, weighted with the scent of earth, stone and water. That night we returned to Huispar, with word that the Mouth to the Underworld had been rediscovered and that we intended to explore it.

"If there was air moving it means the caves are deep," a Tiso man named Der Ab Vyul said. He was new to

Huispar, an overseer at the Ven's latest timber mill.

Catar Ven Ottan, the other overseer, nodded in agreement. The Hautlyren with us were mute, unmoving. The youth with shining eyes, glistening with excitement, while the elders, including my father, were expressionless in a way that I knew connoted disapproval. We were all gathered at the square at the center of town, sipping at cups of beer or coffee.

Around us, couples wandered among the trees of the square, whispering arm in arm. Children played as well, running to and fro, chattering like the gathering blackbirds in the trees above. Their clamor grew as the dusk settled into darkness. It was an evening like any other in Huispar. The crowds would dissipate as the night took hold and everyone returned to their homes for their evening meals.

"In Lysel they have an explorer's club that leads expeditions into the local caves. Perhaps you could form one here. In one they discovered paintings on the walls of mammoths and tigers." Der Ab Vyul said.

"Would you help us?" Jasryl said eagerly and the Tiso man assented.

On the way home my father muttered darkly that all we would find were bones, all that remained of the souls that the cave had eaten.

The lantern came to life at last, its flame, sputtering in the breeze, but holding steady. I lifted it above my head to get clear look at my surroundings. As we had discovered on our first sortie within the Mouth, there was a steep descent just beyond the entrance of the cave. The walls curved into the mountain so I could not even estimate how far down it went. From what I could see, the tunnel was not narrow so I could easily pass through. Though the incline was sharp, it was not so steep that I would require the use of the rope I carried to make my way down. The breeze remained steady as well, suggesting that the passage would take me somewhere.

Feeling reassured, I started below, setting the lantern on the hook on my chest. I had to turn myself to the side, proceeding foot over foot, while leaning back, with my hands out against the surrounding rock, to ensure I kept my balance. I went slowly, knowing that one false step could send me tumbling below and leave me trapped in the Mouth with a broken leg and no hope of rescue. Something similar had no doubt befallen Jasryl.

Why had he done something so foolhardy as to come here by himself? I knew why, of course, and I could not blame him.

We had been friends so long I hardly remember a time when we were not at one another's sides. How many afternoons had we spent exploring the mountains and the cloud forest above Huispar? It had consumed us. At first it had been aimless, the childhood joy of exploration, of seeing new and wondrous things, pushing us on. Lately though, our expeditions had become just that, with all the purpose the name implied. We wanted to reclaim our land, reclaim our past, and, in doing so, stake a claim to our future and the future of all Hautlyren in Niedellun.

Such ideas felt pathetic now that I was descending into the Mouth, faced with the vastness of the caves, as massive as the mountain they were a part of. That it was my fault Jasryl was here, lost and alone, only furthered my sense of insignificance. How could I feel as though I might change the world itself, when I could not even stay loyal to my friend and my principles? It was my betrayal that had sent him here alone and now had me following him, in spite of my growing disquiet.

After perhaps an hour of painstaking effort the cave leveled off and the going became much easier. The path forward twisted and curved, becoming so narrow at points I had to take off the lantern and the rope I had coiled around my back in order to squeeze through. There were branches off the main passage, but I ignored most of them, as they were either too small or obviously led nowhere. Jasryl, I felt certain, would not have taken these false trails.

I had not heard his voice since first entering the caverns and I wondered at that. Had he grown tired of calling? Had he perished from whatever injuries he had suffered? I considered calling out to him, but something held me back. I knew there was no truth to any of the old tales of demons and supernatural creatures that inhabited these places, that there was nothing sacred to them. Still, I could not help feeling I was trespassing in some manner, and I did not want to disturb whatever might lie asleep here. Even if it were only a bat, though, strangely, I had seen none.

The weight of the mountain seemed to sit upon me the farther in I went, awesome and terrifying in equal measure, especially as the passage narrowed again. The walls became jagged with rock formations that seemed to sprout forth, like buds forming into flowers. Water seeped at odd angles from the stone, and I was left utterly soaked and frozen to the core. At times I could hear more water running in the distance, and I found myself imagining that the mountain was alive, as my ancestors believed, and that I was adrift in the sea of its innards, moving from organ to organ on the current of its lifeblood.

It was difficult to keep such thoughts from my mind, to not see the shadows moving in the darkness beyond the glow cast by my lantern, and to believe that the mountain was marshaling its infernal forces against me. The silence itself seemed ominous, a sign that something was lying in wait, preparing. No wonder people went mad in these places, I thought. My own grasp on sanity felt very tenuous indeed.

Just as I began to contemplate turning around and making my way back to the surface, unable to bear being underground a moment longer, the voice sounded again.

"Help me. I'm trapped."

It was as though it had sensed my growing despair, my

increasing claustrophobia, and the repeating thought in my head that I should flee this awful place where I would only find doom. It did not sound like Jasryl, I thought. It sounded inhuman, one of those creatures of myth that draws the unsuspecting to their ruin. I stopped in my tracks, the passage in front of me looking more uncertain.

"Help me. I'm trapped."

This time it sounded more like Jasryl, though he was so frightened as to be almost unrecognizable. I shivered, whether from the cold that had seeped into my bones or terror I could not say. My entire being cried at me to turn around, to go back to the sun and never set foot in this dark and awful place again.

"Help me, please. I'm trapped."

He sounded so near, a chamber or two away, hidden by the darkness and the twisting nether regions of the mountain. I had to go, I realized with a sinking stomach, I could not abandon him. Setting my shoulders and steadying my breath, I pressed on.

"I forbid you to go into those caves again, Kasuir," my father told me the next morning.

"Why not?" I said, bridling at his command. "You are the one who is always saying we must become like the Ven and the Tiso if we are ever to be free of their rule. They had curiosity, they were explorers. If we do not know our own lands, how can we hope to reclaim them?"

"They were conquerors," my father said, with a dismissive nod. He despised and admired the Ven in equal proportion, thinking them depraved and bloodthirsty or enlightened and learned when it suited his purpose.

"Then we must reconquer what is rightfully ours." I said, slapping my fist in my hands.

My mother shushed me as she brought coffee to the table for both of us. She was always worried someone would overhear our discussions and that my father would lose his position as cataman in Huispar, which afforded us much prestige among the Hautlyren.

My father shook his head. "You are too young to understand. There is no future without the Ven now. We are yoked to them completely. Do not return to the cave. There is only the past there."

I opened my mouth to protest further, but he silenced me with a glare and I understood that the matter was closed. Though I often argued with my father, I knew from hard experience that there was a line after which he would accept no dispute. It varied from day to day, depending on his mood, but today it had been reached. I was not to discuss the cave with him, nor was I to explore it, no matter how I might want to.

Though bitterly disappointed, I accepted my father's decision. To defy him was to defy the cataman of Huispar. In a town as small as ours, even the most insignificant act of defiance would be known and would see him lose standing in the eyes of the Hautlyren. Ours was a precarious position, given that we had power in this village, but were beholden to the Ven for it. Many in town sneered behind backs, even as they bowed to our faces. As a result, my father bristled at the least of sleights from anyone, let alone one from his own son.

The next time I saw Jasryl, two days later, he still talked of nothing but the cave, wanting to meet with Der Ab Vyul that evening to establish our explorer's club and plan an expedition. He was talking so quickly his words were out of order, his soft eyes glistening with excitement. I explained to him that I could not, that my father had forbade me to return to the cave.

He flew into a rage at my words, accusing me of all manner of vile cowardice. "You talk and talk of rebellion, but before your father you are a mewling kitten," he said, slamming his fist on the table of beer hall we were in, drawing the stares of the other mid-afternoon customers.

I glared at him and hissed. "What would you have me do then? If I defy my father he will not let me leave

Huispar. Would you have me do that?"

"Your father is not your master. You can leave and there is nothing he can do to stop you."

"Fine," I said. "I can leave. What then? I have no money and I know no one. What would I gain by throwing aside my father?"

Jasryl shook his head. "You think like a slave. Don't you see that all that you have now is by the grace of the Ven. And they can take it from you like that, whether you obey your father or not. If you disobey him you might be left with little or nothing, but at least you would know it was yours."

I stared at Jasryl, my face going flush with anger, for I knew he was right. I was a coward. My father was a servant to the Ven, and I, in spite of all my talk, was unwilling to defy him or them, for fear of losing the prestige it allowed me.

"I will not disobey my father," I said firmly, though I could not meet his eyes.

Jasryl slammed his fists on the table again. "You know Der Ab Vyul will not help in forming the club if you are not involved. You are the only reason he even speaks to me."

"Ah," I said, twisting my own dagger in. "Who is beholden to our overseers now?"

My blow hit its mark, for Jasryl sent his chair clattering to the floor in his haste to stand and leave. "I will be at the Mouth of the Underworld tomorrow, ready to explore it, if you care to join me," he said. "We can only suffer the bonds of our past for so long, soon enough we all must decide whether or not we will be free."

With that he left, leaving me to finish my beer alone under the curious gaze of everyone else in the beer hall.

The passage narrowed again to a second fissured mouth, so thin I was unsure I could even slip through it. I could hear the thunder of water cascading beyond it. I unhooked the lantern from my chest and slung the rope from my shoulder, laying them both within reach of the fissure, so I could pull them through once I had managed to get past. I had to duck my head and contort my whole frame to make my way, scraping myself against the rock. I almost turned back as I went, suddenly filled with the certainty that the stone was pressing down and crushing me and I would be ground to nothing and swallowed.

But the fissure widened slightly so that eventually I was able to crouch on my hands and knees and reach back to pull the lantern and rope through. The roaring of the waterfall was deafening on this side of the fissure, the spray hitting my face as it ricocheted off the cave walls. Spray from the waterfall hit my face and the roar from its fall was deafening.

How had Jasryl's words reached me through such a din? It did not seem possible. A trick of the caves no doubt, sound travelling through caverns I was not able to. Or was it something more ominous?

Lifting the lantern level with my head, while trying to shield it from the water, I saw that I stood on the edge of a precipice, a cavernous dark below where the tumbling water disappeared. I shuddered with vertigo, nausea twisting my stomach. It was a miracle I had not gone over the edge. Just one more step and I would have.

Was this what had befallen Jasryl? Was he lying below, dazed and broken? It seemed unlikely, given the cries I had heard, which surely would have been drowned out by the tumbling water here. As I leaned forward, trying to cast the glare of the lantern a little further into that darkness, I saw the rope he had tied off a little further down the ledge which he had used to make his way to whatever lay below.

I stared at the rope for a long time, tension paralyzing me. It was the first, definitive sign I had found that Jasryl was in fact here. Part of me still thought the voice was nothing more than my guilt playing tricks on me. Now there could be no doubt. Jasryl had come this far and had not returned. I ignored the heavy foreboding that seemed about to swallow me and crept forward to the rope and began to propel myself down the ledge into the darkness.

As I climbed, I tried to stay out of the path of the waterfall, to no avail. The chamber was too small, and I was left even more drenched and chilled than I had been before. Soon the rope was wet as well, leaving it slick and my grip unstable. Each step was precarious, my footholds just as treacherous as the rope. It was only a matter of time before I slipped and crashed into the face of the ledge, nearly shattering my lantern in the process. As I frantically twisted myself to avoid that impending disaster, I caused another, putting the lantern directly into the water's flow, extinguishing its light.

As I clung to rope, scrabbling with my feet for any kind of foothold, I cursed Jasryl fervently for attempting this descent. He was a damned fool and deserved all that fate had given him. I continued to swing in and out of the waterfall and I was quickly left shivering from the frigid water. I could not last long in these conditions, I realized, without falling or succumbing to the cold and a burst of resolve seized me. A moment later I regained my foothold and rapidly scaled down the rest of the ledge, ignoring the water as it cascaded on me.

The cavern remained narrow at the bottom and I had to press myself against the wall to escape from the spray of the water. My arms ached from the effort of descending and I was shivering uncontrollably from the icy cold of the water. How, I wondered, was I going to climb back up, especially if I had to somehow carry an injured Jasryl with me? Jasryl's rope, I estimated, was close to one hundred feet and the end was in my hands. It was impossible.

It took all my strength of will to steady myself so that I could assess the situation rationally and determine how to proceed. First I tried to relight the lantern, but it was hopelessly waterlogged, and I could not see well enough to have any chance of drying it out. As I fumbled with the lantern, it suddenly occurred to me that I was not standing in a pool of water, which meant it had to be going somewhere.

Setting the lantern on the driest spot I could find, I ducked into the water's flow and felt around until I discovered a narrow hole through which all the water emptied. It was far too narrow for me to pass through, which meant Jasryl must have left through some other passage. After a few moments scrabbling I found it: a slender and twisting passage that branched off from the tiny cavern I was in, seeming to run parallel with the flowing water.

Setting my lantern on its hook I began to crawl. My progress forward was excruciating, for it was entirely by feel. Though I wanted nothing more than to rush ahead, in the hopes that the passage widened somewhat, I had to go slowly, for fear that I would find myself at another precipice, or worse. I kept my eyes closed, muttering to myself to stay calm, trying to think about Jasryl and not the various sorts of doom that lay ahead.

After half an hour of twisting and scraping, my hand brushed against something that was not rock. I froze in terror, my hand still upon whatever I was touching. Visions of some beast, deep in slumber, being roused by my stray hand, filled my thoughts, until it dawned on me that what I was touching was metal and glass, quite inanimate, and almost certainly Jasryl's lantern. He must have left it here to dry, I thought, excitement and worry warring within me as I fumbled with my flint to see if I could get the lantern lit.

On my third try the spark caught the oil and flame flickered, illuminating my constricted surroundings. The passage, narrow and narrowing further ahead, went on far beyond where the lantern cast its glow. I shuddered at the sight of it. Better to be blind and fumbling in the darkness than to go forward with the knowledge that I would be crawling into, what in all likelihood, would be my tomb.

I burst into tears, great sobs racking my shoulders, which scraped against the walls of the cave. A moment later the voice came again.

"Help me. I'm trapped. Please come."

"Jasryl," I shouted at the unmoving darkness. "Jasryl, where are you?"

"Help me, Kasuir. Help me."

The evening following my argument with Jasryl, when the men gathered in the square in the dying of the day, he was not among them. The talk was largely about the coming rains, which would render the forest roads impassable and cease all tree cutting in the cloud forest for the next few months. The overseers would return to their homes for the season, or leisure in the highlands, before returning again. Der Ab Vyul was excited about his return home to Yurital where he hoped to arrange a marriage.

"You should come with me," he said to me. My father's face darkened at his words. "I can introduce you to some people, merchants and that sort. Good contacts to have if you are to go anywhere in the world."

I was excited beyond measure at his suggestion, which was the answer to all my dreams. To set foot on the railroad and journey from this town, on the edge of nowhere, to the heart of Niedellun. And to be taken on this adventure by Der Ab Vyul, who had shown himself to be a kind and learned man was beyond what I could ever have imagined.

"Our kind are not welcomed in the homes of merchants in Yurital," my father said in a disapproving tone.

"On the contrary," Der Ab Vyul said, "any man with a head about him can make his way in that world. Oh, there will be some who look down on him as a Hautlyrun, but you can find that here as well. And there are others who are more, shall we say, civilized. Those are the homes I would be taking him into."

My father murmured something polite to Der Ab Vyul, but I could tell he was unconvinced. Having risen to his position, he was intimately aware of how precarious the rise of any Hautlyrun in Niedellun was. He could never believe that we would be accepted into the homes of the Ven, unless it was to do the chores of the house.

"I would be glad for the opportunity," I said, pointedly looking at my father. His face turned even darker, but he did not argue the point, which I counted as a victory. Given time, I might be able to bring him to my side.

In my excitement following Der Ab Vyul's offer, I forgot all about Jasryl's absence, returning home to dreams of walking the teeming streets of Yurital. The next day I was kept busy running various errands for my mother, so that it was late in the day when I had time for myself and my thoughts strayed to Jasryl. I decided to find him, to see if he had been daring enough to go to the cave without me. I suspected not. For all his talk, he was as cowardly as I. Part of me wanted to force him to admit to it after all his bravado.

I went to all the places he was likely to be, but he was nowhere to be found. Worse, no one had seen him that day or the day before. I called on his family to see if they had seen him, or knew where he was.

"He left yesterday to go into the forest for a hike," his mother told me. "He said might be a few days. I assumed you had gone with him."

Fear hardened in my chest and it was difficult to breath, let alone speak. "What did he take with him?" I managed to say at last.

She frowned, sensing my concern. "Food, a lantern and some candles, and a rope."

I do not know how long it took to compose myself, but when I had at last managed to, I retreated back to the edge of the cavern the waterfall passed through. There I left my lantern to dry, hoping it would be fine by the time I returned with Jasryl, so that I could use it to illuminate the cavern while I climbed to the ledge. If I could manage to keep the other lantern from the water when I climbed, I would be able to light the rest of my way out of the cave. How I was going to carry Jasryl as I climbed was a question I did not dare to consider. I would simply have to find a way.

The walls seemed to scrape and tear at me as I returned down the passage and pressed on toward Jasryl's voice. I was left bruised and a little bloodied, my clothes torn, before I had gone far. Jasryl's words rang in my ears, drawing me on further, in spite of these difficulties.

He was nearby now, to judge by the sound, the fear and hurt plainly evident in his voice. I tried not to think about the state I might find him in or whether my efforts might all be in vain.

The passage began a steep descent, and as I fought to stop myself from sliding down into that oblivion, a foul odor became apparent, growing stronger the father I went. It was a combination of decay and rotting flesh, mixed with a sulfurous gas, which seared the membranes in my nostrils. I stopped where I was, debating whether or not I should continue on. If the gas was poisonous, I was already doomed, I reasoned.

"Help me, Kasuir. I'm trapped."

I jumped at the sound of his voice, cracking my head on the rock above me. It caused me to lose my balance and I slid forward, scraping myself painfully on the rocks, until I managed to get myself halted. It sounded as though he were right beside me.

"I'm coming Jasryl," I called out, in what I hoped was a reassuring tone.

I pulled a handkerchief from my pockets, covering my nose and mouth, in the hopes of dispelling some of the putrid stench. It had little effect and my eyes were soon streaming with tears.

The cave itself began to change as I went forward, the

rock surfaces becoming damper, making my progress ever more precarious. Everything was warmer, including the air, which was suddenly heavy with humidity. I began to feel dizzy as well, a side effect of the nauseating smell, I was certain.

"Help me. I'm trapped. Kasuir."

The voice seemed to surround me, echoing around the narrow passage behind me. He had to be right here. I contorted myself so that I could peer behind me, pressing myself against one of the passages walls. There was no one there. Just a trick of the caves, I told myself, trying to steady my breathing.

My panic only grew moments later as I had to fight to dislodge myself from the walls. Trails of mucus came with where the walls had tried to cling to me. The rock had changed I realized, as I touched it hesitantly, becoming firm, yet porous. When I pressed against them my fingers left marks. Holding them up to the lantern light I saw that the mucus was clear like water, just as these walls were the color of stone.

A puff of malodourous air gusted up the chamber, blinding me with its stench, as a sinking realization began to settle in. I was in something that was alive. The Mouth of the Underworld was real and I was in it. I turned to flee.

"Help me, Kasuir. I'm trapped."

It was Jasryl's voice but it was not. I stumbled forward, fear clenching at my throat, my hands and knees getting stuck with each movement. The passage seemed to close in around me and I was sent sprawling. I thrashed out blindly, trying to free myself so that I could begin to crawl again, but it was no use. The lantern went dark a moment later. Something in the air had changed and the flame could no longer burn.

I continued to struggle, but it was to no effect. Numbness began to spread across my limbs and chest. In desperation, though I knew no one was there to rescue me, I cried out.

"Help me. I'm trapped."

Everything began to slow and the darkness deepened. Soon I could no longer even struggle or feel my body. Only my mind seemed aware of what was occurring, though that awareness was dim and distant. The last thing I heard was my own voice echoing around me, up the unseen passages to the mouth above.

"Help me. I'm trapped."

SLAVISH ADHERENT

THE TWENTIETH GRADATION

If it were given to him to do again, Hector forever asked himself, would he still make the same fatal error? According to all the Reconciliations of his Audits of Faith, he would. It was his basic nature, as a Slavish Adherent of the Twentieth Gradation, an inescapable result of who he was and his place in the world. Though Hector would never be so bold as to question the Tenets of the Faith, part of him did wonder whether something so inadvertent, a moment's inattention and no more, could possibly define anyone, let alone someone as loyal and true as he knew himself to be. But it did. The Faith was exacting, after all, allowing no room for doubt or weakness. He had already demonstrated he had an ample supply of both, given his allocation as a Twentieth Gradation, an inauspicious ranking if ever there was one.

The error occurred the first morning of the Reimbursements, when every Slavish Adherent brought their most recent Reconciliation to their Lead Adherent for review and the dispensation of the faith. Hector was in a jubilant mood for, not only had his last Reconciliation been glowing, he had discovered certain discrepancies in his department's Audit—specifically the duplication of some procurements of Faith—which, if rectified, would result in a significant savings. Such matters were always looked upon kindly by Lead Adherents, for the Faith was very clear on the sinfulness of waste.

The Lead Adherent welcomed Hector into his office with his usual bonhomie, clasping his hand firmly and wringing it, and offering him a beaming, unrelenting smile that always left Hector uncomfortable. They rarely spoke outside of the monthly Reimbursements, unless the Lead Adherent had a task for him to complete, so it was always strange to Hector that he should greeted with the warmth due the dearest of colleagues, when they were no more than passing acquaintances. It was insincere, Hector thought, but would never dare to say, for to do so would to imply that the Lead Adherent was acting falsely, a sin of two gradations, not to be issued lightly.

"Welcome...Hector," the Lead Adherent said, hesitating as always when he came to his name, and gestured for him to sit. "You have your Reconciliation for the month I presume."

Hector nodded affirmatively, feeling both nervous and excited, for even in that moment he understood that this Reimbursement would change the course of his life. How right he was, and how he wished he had never been so great a fool. Still smiling, the smile never seemed to leave his face, the Lead Adherent asked him to proceed and he did, cautiously at first, stumbling here and there, but gaining in strength and conviction as he went.

He outlined the discrepancies he had discovered in the Audit, the duplicated procurements, always involving the same three Cardinal Conglomerates and the same service requests which, as he noted, he could not confirm had ever actually been rendered in any of the cases. As he explained to the Lead Adherent, "The savings involved in reconciling these discrepancies would be considerable. And, if we pursue the procurement errors, there might be even further reconciliations to be made. I am more than happy to continue to demonstrate my adherence to the Protocols of the Faith in this area."

He had expected to be greeted with a flourish of praise from the Lead Adherent. This had always been the case with his previous Reimbursements, all of which had been meager by comparison to this one. But though the Lead Adherents smile remained firmly in place throughout his Reconciliation, Hector thought he noticed a slight strain beginning to show on his cheeks and a dimming in the gleam of his eyes. When he finished, the Lead Adherent stood and ushered him from the office without offering any praise or congratulations, or pronouncing on his Reimbursement for the month. All he would say to Hector was that he would need to discuss the matter further with the Senior Adherent.

That was hardly regular procedure, but Hector was unconcerned. The discovery of this kind of discrepancy demanded action on the part of any Lead Adherent, and he would want to ensure that the Senior Adherent was apprised of what was occurring before taking any action. The Senior Adherent arrived less than an hour later and was ushered into the Lead Adherent's office where they conducted a hushed conference. After a short time the Lead Adherent emerged and beckoned for Hector to join them. He was not smiling.

Nor did the Senior Adherent look any happier when Hector entered. He was told to sit, which he did, while the Senior Adherent studied him, a grim expression on his face. The Lead Adherent, standing behind his superior, looked pained as he stared over Hector's shoulder. Hector looked from face to face and swallowed, feeling sweat starting to form on his lip.

"Is there something wrong?" he ventured, as the silence lingered.

"I understand you claim to have uncovered some auditing discrepancies," the Senior Adherent said, his tone implying that Hector could not be more wrong.

"Yes, I have. As I was saying to…"

"You have committed a grave offense, Slavish Adherent," the Senior Adherent intoned gravely.

Hector looked from one man to the other, feeling utterly flabbergasted. What offense had he committed?

"Your sin is vanity, to think that you, a Slavish Adherent of the Twentieth Gradation would be capable of discerning such discrepancies, that you claim exist, when neither myself nor the Lead Adherent, who are far more versed in the intricacies of the auditing regime, were able to note them. Do you truly claim to know the protocols of the faith better than us?"

Hector blinked, his world falling away before him. "No, I—" he began to say.

The Lead Adherent cut him off. "There is no excuse for this perfidy. You almost as much as accused me of creating the discrepancies myself." The Senior Adherent glanced at the Lead Adherent and they shared a look, the latter falling silent.

"I would never dare to presume to accuse either of you of wrongdoing," Hector protested. "The discrepancies are real though. The procurements have been duplicated."

The Senior Adherent shook his head. "I am afraid you are incorrect." He pulled out the balance sheet, an arcane list of credits and debits, protocols and other ephemera, all designed to better augment the Conglomerate's share of the Faith, pointing to the three procurements Hector had discovered the duplications in. "As you can see," he said, "There is no duplication."

Hector opened and closed his mouth. Everyone knew the balance sheet was used only to show to those outside the Conglomerate, to ensure their proper share of praise and investment, and that the truth lay in the auditing forms. Not that the Conglomerate filed false balance sheets. To do so would be against the Protocols of the Faith, but exaggerations and the like were to be expected. He could not comprehend why the Senior Adherent was not referring to the auditing forms. The Slavish Adherents were all expected to use the forms for their reconciliations.

"But the auditing documents—" he began to say.

"Are irrelevant in this matter," the Senior Adherent said. He sighed and rubbed his eyes. "This attitude of yours is most troubling, I'm afraid. It has been my understanding, based on the reports of your Lead Adherent, as well as your reconciliations, that you were a compliant and loyal Slavish Adherent. Your actions in your Reimbursement, and in our meeting today, are unbecoming, both of a Slavish Adherent of the Twentieth Gradation and of somebody who works in this office."

Hector felt lightheaded and feared he might vomit, or break into tears in front of both of them. He knew what was coming next, even before it was said.

"Your failure to adhere to the Protocols of the Faith is troubling in the extreme. We cannot have someone of that ilk working in this Conglomerate. The Faith is too important."

"I have always been faithful," Hector managed to say.

The Senior Adherent waved his objections aside. "Yes, there is no doubt, to this point, that you have been a model Adherent. This will be taken into consideration when I make my recommendation for termination. Given your efforts here over the years, I will strongly recommend that you be terminated at the Twenty-Fifth Gradation of the faith. Good day Slavish Adherent."

The Senior Adherent stood, signaling the conclusion of the interview. Dazed, Hector got to his feet and, to his own humiliation, shook both the Senior Adherent and Lead Adherent's hands. He left the room and went to sit at his desk, forgetting that he had been terminated. An internal chime sounded in his ear, notifying him of a new message in his Penance to be reconciled before he could be given Absolution. Opening it using his retinal implant, his field of vision was filled with the notification that his termination had been approved. A second message from the Hierarchy informed him that Reconciliation was complete, and for his Reimbursement he had been indebted five gradations and would thereafter be assessed at the Twenty-Fifth Gradation. He was still there reading both messages half an hour later when two Adherents from security arrived to escort him from the premises.

THE TWENTY-FIFTH GRADATION

Hector did not know how long he wandered the streets, bereft of purpose and unable to even think, before he returned to his home, but it was well after dark. The air in the city was cool and the streets around his building were quiet. He came to the door of his apartment building and keyed in his code. The display screen blinked and informed him his code had been denied. He tried again and received the same message. A third time produced no change in the outcome. Finally, he pressed the key for the manager. A series of beeps informed him he was on hold. They dropped away, leaving a faint static, and a distant voice said, "Yes?"

"It's Hector," he said. "My code isn't working for some reason."

There was a long pause on the other end, long enough that Hector almost dialed again thinking the call must have been dropped. The building manager cleared his throat. "Your lease in the building has been terminated under section 3.1 of the agreement you signed. Notification has been sent to your ocular. Please refer to it for further details. I have arranged for your possessions to be made available for pick up at the nearest Confessional tomorrow beginning at seven am, as per section 3.1.a. Your possessions will remain available for 48 hours, as per the agreement, at which point they will be auctioned off and the reimbursement applied to the building repair fund."

Hector only listened to the first part of what the manager said, drifting away from the building as the reality of his situation fully settled in. He checked his ocular as he went and saw that a notification of his eviction had been sent. As a Slavish Adherent of the Twenty-Fifth Gradation, he was no longer welcome in the apartment complex, as all tenants had to be Adherents of the Twenty-First Gradation or higher. This clause was in the lease agreement of just about every domicile in the city, because it was understood that any Adherent below the Twenty-First Gradation could not possibly have any legal means of employment.

As he reflected on that, Hector realized, with a growing despair, the enormity of his current predicament. Not only had he been thrown out of his domicile, he had no way of acquiring a new one, except through illicit means. All his assets, including the meager savings he managed to gain from the Reimbursements he had received over the last twelve years he had been working at the Conglomerate, as well as the pittance his father had given him upon his Independence Day, would be frozen. No financial institution would want to do business with a Slavish Adherent of such questionable gradation. Even his parents would be reluctant to help him. It would be better for them to disassociate with him, given his new status. And in truth, he did not want to bring his troubles to them. They had enough difficulties as it was, given his father was only an Adherent of the Nineteenth Gradation and had many years of work ahead of him, without assuming the debts his son had incurred.

No, it seemed best that Hector deal with this situation on his own. But how? Adherents of the Twenty-Fifth Gradation were known to be of low repute, irreconcilables, given to theft and other illicit activity. Those were the only avenues that lay open to him. If he were somehow successful enough in those endeavors, he might gain enough money to buy his way back to a higher gradation. Money was no sin after all, regardless of how it was gained. But he knew nothing of thievery, nothing of the trade in illicit materials. The people who trafficked in such things were born into it, just as he had been born into his undistinguished life in the audit branch of one of the larger Conglomerates in the Imperium.

He wandered the streets for hours, bereft, and having no idea where he should go. Hunger at last forced him into an eatery where he used half of his remaining cash reserves to buy a warm meal, which he ate slowly, savoring each bite as though it were his last. It very well might be, he thought, despair gripping his whole body. He had to leave the eatery before it overwhelmed him, and he continued his aimless perambulations through the darkened streets of the Imperium. There he felt lost and anonymous, his shame hidden by the shadows.

It was a ruse though, to believe such a thing. Anyone who encountered him would quickly and easily be able to verify his gradation level by using their ocular. There was no hiding; he had to embrace his new identity, the Tenets of the Faith required it. There was no better time than to do so tonight, he decided. Buoyed by that resolution he set off immediately for one of the city's wealthier districts, Paradise, where Adherents of the tenth rank or higher lived.

Most of these were gated compounds, kept by Slavish Adherents of lower gradations (though more highly ranked than Hector himself had ever been), for these were the rulers of the Imperium, the most exalted of the Faith. Those above the Fifth Gradation did not even receive Reimbursements or suffer through Reconciliations. Their Faith had transcended such profane concerns. The unreconciled, of which he could now count himself among, rarely ventured into such areas and never without suspicion being cast upon them.

Everyone, though, had heard of irreconcilables who had conducted daring raids upon the compounds of the elite, making away with unimaginable Reimbursements that they used to fund their own rise up the gradation scale. The thought of that gave him some hope. As the Protocols of the Faith made clear, those who dedicated themselves to the Faith, regardless of gradation, would receive their just reward. Even an irreconcilable could receive Reimbursement.

As he strolled down various streets, he glanced from compound to compound, trying to judge whether any would be good targets for a novice thief. They all looked to be heavily fortified, with electrified walls and extensive surveillance that he would be hard pressed to thwart. The entire enterprise began to seem foolhardy, and he was about to abandon it and head to the slums to see if he could find somewhere to spend the night and start anew in the morning, when he noticed a small compound sitting dark amidst the light of the rest.

He approached it cautiously, looking about to see if anyone was watching. The telltale hum of electrical equipment that seemed to fill every empty thought of his life was strangely absent. He tried the door to the compound gate and discovered that it was unlocked and he stepped within, scurrying up the winding path to the house. It was dark as well, the main door open. Hector crept within, conscious of the shuffle of his footsteps upon the carpet. Silence reigned, except for his strained breathing and the pounding of his heart, as he tried to feel his way through the dark.

After stumbling into a wall he managed to locate a light switch and turned it on, though he knew it might alert anyone in the compound to his presence. The stillness persisted, the lights revealing a room of unimaginable splendor. There were hand carved, darkly stained pieces of furniture that he was afraid to touch, paintings that he dimly recognized as the works of Master Adherents on the walls, and various antiques and other knickknacks, each one as valuable as his entire domicile. None of it, he realized immediately, was worth taking. They were all too unique, too easily traced, for him to be able to sell and get even a portion of their value.

He felt sick to his stomach at the sight of it all, the enormity of the difficulty that lay before him settling upon his shoulders. But he had no choice, he told himself. If he was to be a Faithful Adherent, as the Doctrines of the Faith said he must, he needed to apply himself to those tasks befitting his gradation.

The rest of the main floor was much the same, ostentatious and ornate, magnificent and vast. With the silence hanging over everything, he felt as though he were in a place of worship, not a habitation. His every step seemed to disturb the equilibrium, carefully established by the rituals he was not holy enough to witness. And still nothing he saw looked worth the effort of stealing, though the wealth on display was almost incalculable, and he was tempted to abandon the attempt entirely.

Instead he forced himself to go upstairs, hoping that there might be some valuables that he could find, though he feared they would be locked in a safe, which he did not know how to break into. He was still wrestling with the question of what to do in that event, as he walked into the first darkened room off the stairway and was greeted by a terrified shriek. Light followed the cry, blinding him momentarily. When his vision came back into focus, he saw a woman, flimsily dressed in an exquisite negligee of silk or some other fabulous material, cowering before him, her fists raised as though she were ready to do battle.

"Who are you?" she said, her voice hoarse with fear, before her ocular informed her of his identity.

His own device informed him that she was Abigail Miranda, Fourth Gradation of the Faith. Hector found himself holding his breath, looking upon her with wonder. It was not just her very evident beauty that inspired such emotion in him. It was the fact that he had never before been in the presence of one of the Transcended, the holiest of all Adherents to the Faith. Here she was, an angel in truth, her skin and face without flaw, and, even in this moment of panic, not a hair out of place.

She seemed to reach the same conclusion as he moments later. "You shouldn't be seeing me. You are irreconcilable. What are you doing here?"

Hector cleared his throat and said, apologetically, "I am here to rob you blind."

"How horrible," she said, revulsion in her voice. She looked him up and down with some interest, which gave him pause.

"I'm afraid I'll have to restrain you while I do my work here," he said. "Can't have you interfering. I'll need you to tell me where you keep the valuables as well."

"How awful," she said. "There's rope on the bed."

He nodded his thanks and went to the bed, where there was indeed a coil of rope laid out. Why, he wondered, would she have this at hand in her bedroom?

She wrinkled her nose as he turned to her, rope in hand. "You're quite polite for an irreconcilable. Have you been at the Twenty Fifth Gradient long?"

"No," he said, as he came up beside her, inhaling her scent. "I was Twentieth Gradation until this afternoon."

"Pity," she said with a sigh. "Well, you'll have to do."

A stun device materialized in her hand and, before he had time to react, she shoved it against his chest sending an electrical pulse through him and he fell to the floor senseless.

THE THIRTIETH GRADATION

The first thing Hector became aware of when he regained consciousness was that his head felt as though it had been split in two. His vision was a swirl of light when he managed to open his eyes. The second was that his clothes had been removed from his person and he was quite naked. The third was that his arms were bound by the rope Abigail Miranda had offered him to use to secure her, and that he was hanging from that rope, which had been looped through a ring that extended from the ceiling above. The fourth was that Abigail Miranda was sitting watching him on the edge of her bed, still wearing the negligee that both revealed and concealed her exquisite form.

She smiled as she saw that he was awake and said, "Your head doesn't hurt too much I hope? Good. I've reported you for violating my virtue, I'm afraid, which means you've been reassessed at the Thirtieth Gradation of the Faith."

Hector flinched at her words and the room began to swim again and he worried he would vomit. When he had recovered somewhat he managed to check his ocular and saw that, indeed, a message had been sent announcing his reduction to the Thirtieth Gradation. Strangely, there was no further message indicating that the police had been called to arrest him for his supposed violation of an Adherent of the Third Gradation.

"But I have not violated you," he said in protest. "I only intended to rob you, not to harm your person."

"It's better this way, don't you think?" she said. "The unreconciled savage violating the property of the Adherent, and then her purity as well. He cares nothing for the rules and society, the propriety of the Adherents. She manages to fight him off and even secure him for arrest…"

"But you have not called the police," Hector said.

"…but those bonds will not hold him long and he will overpower her. For he must, it is his nature. She will resist and be horrified naturally, but part of her will welcome it, even desire it."

As she spoke, her hand strayed to her throat and her ample chest began to rise and fall in excitement. Hector stared at her in wonder, unsure how he was supposed to react, for he had never imagined a Transcendent acting in this fashion.

"I am just here to rob you, as I said. In fact, your door was open, so technically I have not even violated your property. I would never dream of violating your body. That goes against all the Tenets of the Faith, even for an irreconcilable of the Twenty-Fifth Gradation."

She leapt from the bed, approaching him shaking her hands in frustration. "But you have been reassessed at the Thirtieth Gradation. Violating me is expected. The Tenets of the Faith are quite clear on how such lowly Adherents act."

Hector shook his head sadly. "The only reason I am at the Thirtieth Gradation is because you have falsely reported that I violated you. I never thought a Transcendent could do such a thing."

"But you see," she said earnestly, "You have nothing to

lose. You have already been assessed. Why not take some enjoyment from it before I call the police. Embrace your true savage nature."

Hector frowned. "Maybe I can explain to the police that this is all a misunderstanding."

"Oh no," Abigail Miranda said, "Oh no. They will not believe you. How could they? You are of the Thirtieth Gradation and I am of the Fourth. Who is purer of heart?"

Hector saw the truth in what she said and hung his head. There was no escaping his fate. He would be arrested and imprisoned for the his remainder of eternity.

"Break free of your bonds," Abigail Miranda cried out. "Ravish me. Seize the spoils of your degradation."

As she spoke she ran a hand along his neck and down his naked chest, but he was so disconsolate facing the ruins of his life that he failed to notice her entreaties. She sighed and returned to sit on her bed. "I thought men like you were beyond the pale, reprobates and animals."

"I apologize," Hector said. "I am fairly new to the gradation, as I said. Perhaps I just need time find my true nature."

"Yes," she said, excited again, "Yes, you just need time. And why not now? It would be good practice for you. As an Adherent of the Thirtieth Gradation you will be expected to commit such foul deeds again. You need to be prepared."

He could not deny the logic in what she said, and, as with his theft, it was better to embrace his fate than to wallow in sorrow over what he had lost. The Tenets of the Faith were quite clear that one had to accept one's gradation after all, for it reflected his innate being. "Very well," he said to Abigail Miranda, who clapped her hands in delight and adjusted her negligee so that it settled more becomingly on her.

Hector was just about to test the bonds that held him and attempt to break free when a voice sounded behind him. "What the hell is going on here?"

Abigail Miranda leapt from the bed and let out a startled "Oh."

"Why is security down? Why are you dressed like that? And who is this man and why isn't he wearing any clothes?"

The man who was asking these questions stepped from behind Hector and looked from him to Abigail, incredulity and rage straining at the edges of his face. His ocular informed him this was Reginald Miranda, also of the Fourth Gradation, and undoubtedly Abigail's husband.

"By all that is holy," Reginald said, turning his attention to Abigail and ignoring Hector completely. "What are you doing? This man is of the Thirtieth Gradation. He should not even be looking upon us."

There was a pause as he read the latest notices and Hector could see the color drain from his face. "My god, has he violated you? If he has—"

"Not yet," Abigail sniffed, looking very perturbed, "If you hadn't shown up he might have."

"You promised me you wouldn't do this again."

"Oh you made me promise," Abigail said, with a dismissive wave of her hand. "I'm not some icon you can keep on the wall and pay devotion to. If you won't give me what I want I'm going to find it elsewhere."

"From him? He's of the Thirtieth Gradation. He's a predator and thief." Reginald was incredulous.

"At least he was willing to make love to me."

"Is this true?" Reginald rounded to face Hector.

He shrugged apologetically. "I'm an Adherent of the Thirtieth Gradation. I have to adhere to the Tenets of the Faith and my place within them."

Reginald stared at Hector, his mouth quivering apoplectically, before turning back to Abigail. They began to yell at each other, each of them swearing they would do grievous harm to the other, calling each other no better than an Abhorrent of the Fifteenth Gradation and worse. They were completely oblivious of Hector, and, after listening to their argument for several minutes, he realized that he was superfluous to the situation. He tested the rope that bound his hands and found that it was, in fact, very loose and he easily slipped free of it. After collecting his clothes from the floor, he slipped downstairs and put them on. After a lingering look at his immaculate surroundings, he headed back out into the night.

THE THIRTY-SIXTH GRADATION

Hector wandered from Paradise, heading for the worst parts of town, those purgatories where lost souls resided. As he went, his ocular informed him that the police had arrived at the scene of his violation of Abigail Miranda and he was now a fugitive of law. For this failure he had been docked two gradients and been reassessed at the Thirty-Second Gradation, a state of being reserved for murderers, cannibals and other savages of the wild. He had no intention of committing any such acts, at least he did not think so. But as an Adherent was it not his responsibility, in a sense, to embrace who he was? His actions after all had led him to this desperate place, so the fault lay within, it was part of his being.

Soon he found himself in Purgatory, a slum on the outskirts of the city, where he had never set foot before today. Every door seemed to be closed and every window shuttered and no one was upon the streets but him. The streets seemed menacing, though he was utterly alone, threats lurking in every corner and behind every shadow. The wind had a bite to it that made him shiver and he regretted not waiting to claim his goods from the Confessional. Morning was growing near and he did not have time to make his way back there. Not that he could, with the police looking for him.

The realization that morning approached and he had not slept yet made him feel the full weight of the exhaustion he had been trying to ignore. He decided to try to find something that passed for shelter and get what sleep he could, before determining what to do with the remains of his life. It took some time, for though the Purgatory streets were all insinuation and hidden places, none of them ever materialized into anything substantial. The shadows dissipated as he grew close to them, leaving only empty streets with no cover from the elements. At last, he came to a winding stairway that descended so far that he could see no bottom. There seemed to be no purpose to it, other than to lead into some pit or sewer, but he started down it, thinking that, if nothing else, it would keep him out of the wind.

It took him close to half an hour to reach the bottom and by the time he did he was utterly exhausted. The sun was coming above, dim on the horizon, but none of the light reached below. There was only murk and he became afraid that in his exhausted state he would lose his footing and tumble down the remainder of the stairs. So it was with great relief when he descended the final step and found himself on a small circular landing. The landing was empty, but as his eyes adjusted to the gloom, he realized there was a door opposite the staircase.

Hector went to the door, heavy and crafted from wrought iron. The handle was corroded and the door, along with the surrounding stone, looked ancient and weathered. The air smelled of mildew and moss. It seemed clear that no one had been down these stairs and through this door in a very long time. There was no indication of where it might lead, and Hector had no idea himself. It seemed to him that he must be well below even the sewers of the city.

Unsure of how to proceed Hector reached out and

knocked. He could hear the sound reverberating out in what seemed like a vast emptiness beyond the door. Taken aback he hesitated, wondering if he dared try to open the door. A moment later a knock, ponderous and loud, came from the other side. By instinct Hector reached out and tried the doorknob. It was resistant to turning but unlocked, and though the door itself was heavy, the hinges in desperate need of oil, it swung open as he pulled, groaning loudly.

Facing him on the side of the threshold was a vast sea of humanity, beyond number, stretching out beyond sight in a chamber so massive he could not comprehend its proportions. As he looked at the people facing him, Hector realized that they were not people as he was generally used to seeing them. They were all grotesque and monstrous, grimacing and leering in expression, their clothes rags and chains. A putrid stench wafted toward him from the room and he nearly retched.

One of their number, a man carrying a clipboard filled with torn paper that he glanced at, nodding at various intervals, stepped forward, extending a hand to Hector who took it. "Well then," the man said, "Very good. That's done. If you'll just follow me for a moment."

He guided Hector into the chamber and out of the doorway, giving him a distracted smile. As soon as they had both left the doorway, the mass of people began to move forward, streaming out of the chamber and up the stairs, heading toward the city

"What is this place? Who are you people?" Hector said, feeling vaguely that he should be stopping these monstrosities from fleeing what he now thought must be a prison. His ocular seemed not to be functioning here, because it did not inform him of who any of these people might be, or what their gradations were. They would be miserable indeed, perhaps as miserable as his own.

"Hmm," the man said, still distracted by whatever was on his clipboard. "Oh. Well. This is a Pit of Hell. One of them anyway. And we are Abhorrents, mostly of the Fifteenth to the Thirtieth Gradation, you understand. Far from elite. But we do try. Thank you, by the way, for opening the door. Just a huge help, for me especially. It's so difficult to try to keep things orderly when everybody is convinced they're a prince of evil."

Hector felt his mouth go dry and his hands begin to tremble. Association with Abhorrents, and the Hell-bound in general, was forbidden by the Tenets of the Faith. Strictly and plainly and utterly forbidden. Failure to follow this tenet resulted in one being assessed at the Thirty-Sixth Gradation, the lowest of the Adherents, so low in fact that one wasn't really an Adherent at all. One was an Abhorrent. Which apparently he now was. As if to confirm his thoughts, his ocular, which had been recording the faces of those passing by, chimed with a notification informing him that he had been reassessed at the Thirty-Sixth Gradation and had been cast from the faith entirely. He was to proceed immediately to a Pit of Hell, if he was not already there.

"What will they do?" Hector said, more out of politeness than anything else. He would, he realized, never see anyone he knew again after tonight.

"Hmm? Oh. The apocalypse if all goes well. But these things are tricky, you know. You're more than welcome to join us."

Hector shook his head. He wanted only to lie down, to forget everything that had happened this terrible day.

"Suit yourself then," the man said. "Rivers of blood and untold suffering. Quite the sight to see. I wouldn't miss it myself."

Hector shrugged. If he was one of these people now, he should perhaps find out how they lived. "Very well."

"Excellent. You can join the mob whenever you please. I have to stay here to see to the door. Good luck."

Hector drifted over and joined the flow of people, nodding at those he slipped in beside, and headed back into the city. Above it was a glorious sunny day. The Abhorrents spilled out into every street, racing in all directions like a river that had spilled over its banks. They rampaged, setting buildings afire, beating and stabbing anyone they met, stealing anything that wasn't tied down, and destroying anything that wasn't, laughing with glee all the while

Hector mostly followed, staying aside, his heart not in the moment, though one of his fellow Abhorrents gave him a knife to use. He held it uncomfortably, unsure of how to use it and whether he even wanted to. The Faith was clear on the matter, though, he was beyond the pale, cast out. His ocular, after its last notification, had gone silent. This was his place.

As they went down another street, an Adherent approached him, looking confused at all the destruction, the rioting and the fire, the screams of horror and glee.

"What's going on here?"

"Apocalypse," Hector said.

"Damn it," the man said. "This is always such a pain. You can never get anything done."

Hector nodded sympathetically and stabbed the man in the eye.

THE WOMAN WHO DIDN'T SPEAK

There was no light in the sky when Marjiana rose from bed. The red sun—which she had yet to grow used to in the fifteen years she had lived on this planet—remained hidden from sight behind the horizon. It did not feel like home this place. Not even after all this time living here, not to mention the extended journey to arrive at this destination. It was still a place she had come to, not a place she was from.

And also the place she would be spending her remaining days, however many they might be. For there was no leaving here, no matter how much they all might wish to.

That was a thought best not dwelt upon, especially not first thing in the morning, lest it cast a shadow over the rest of the day. There were shadows enough in this place without bringing more into this world. Life was hard enough as it was.

She did not turn on any lights in the house, preferring to move about by feel, and wanting to preserve their reserves of electricity for necessities and emergencies. A splash of cool water on her face after brushing her teeth was the only luxury she allowed herself. That and the coffee she set to boil atop a gas burner . It was not real coffee, but she had mostly forgotten the taste of the real thing. This was near enough, and even the supplies of it were dwindling.

Day by day all their supplies were dwindling. And what would remain when they were gone?

Another thought best put aside. There was a long day's work ahead and Marjiana did not need to join those who had succumbed to the settler's melancholy, remaining in their homes, leaving their fields to ruin, waiting for starvation or the elements to release them from their suffering. Not that it wasn't tempting. But she had four mouths to feed—five if one counted Kjessel, and she supposed she had to. He was her husband, after all.

When the coffee was ready she drank it, savoring each drop, closing her eyes to listen to the stillness around her. Neither Kjessel nor any of her sons were awake, and none of them would be until after the sun rose. None of the neighbors were up and out in the fields either. The quiet— so strange, at first, after a lifetime spent on a planet with birds and insects, or on the vessel that had brought them here, where there had been a constant hum and hiss of systems at work—was now something she treasured above all else.

It was the one thing she would take from this failed world, if she could. Given there was no leaving here, it was her only solace.

She could hear someone stirring in one of the other rooms and, taking that as her signal, she rose from the kitchen table and went out to the fields to begin her day's work.

Garuhj, the hetman, welcomed them all to the main square of the settlement, embracing many of the women and clenching the hands of the men, beaming from ear to ear. He had been elected hetman in the fifth year of the settlement, the first time the crops failed. They had failed twice more since then, to say nothing of the rhesus fevers, which had killed more than half of those in the settlement. Yet his beaming countenance remained unchanged.

Even now, as the crops began to show the first signs of the strange rot that no one could determine the cause of, Garuhj maintained his outward optimism. Marjiana suspected his own thoughts were not so positive, but the hetman was a politician above all, and versed in projecting confidence. She considered him a thing to be suffered, no different than the rot and the fevers, another of the burdens of this place to be endured.

"Welcome Marjiana. Danjiel. Codij. Jeriem. I hope you are all well. Kjessel is not joining the celebration?"

Marjiana shook her head.

"He's not well," Danjiel said, a little too quickly.

The hetman did not notice, his gaze already going beyond them to the next family of settlers he was to greet. In the celebration that followed, Garuhj gave his usual speech, marked by his typical platitudes and his claim that hope was necessary, in spite of all that had gone wrong.

"When we set down on this day, thirteen years ago, it was to an uninhabitable rock. We knew there would be trials and tribulations, and no doubt there have been. Not all of us have survived them, and we would be remiss if we did not remember them. But we need to honor their memory and sacrifice by recognizing what we have achieved, which is so much.

"Where once there was a barren windswept landscape, now there is soil, there is air and there is water. All the necessities we require to survive. Instead of looking at all those places where we have struggled and failed, we should look at what we have achieved, and recognize that we have it in us to survive here."

Garuhj's eyes flashed with emotion as he spoke. He truly believed. But the celebrations that followed were tepid, everyone only too aware of the failures of the colony. For they were in evidence all around them. The cloudless sky that promised no rain yet again. The thin soil they trod upon, from which little could grow, and which seemed to contain the germ of the rot that ate at what did.

Even the food at the celebration was a sign of failure, for it was taken from the ever-dwindling supplies the vessel that had brought them here had carried. Intended to tide them over during the first lean years after the terraforming was complete, they had been unused initially during those bountiful years, only to become absolutely necessary now.

As Marjiana and the boys prepared to take their leave of the celebration and begin the walk back to their home, about a kilometer from the central square of the settlement, Garuhj intercepted them, barely hiding his concern.

"Leaving so soon?" he said. When no one replied, he added, "What's this I hear about you not speaking anymore?"

Marjiana did not reply, shrugging and motioning her one hand slightly in dismissal in reply. The hetman blinked, unsure how to respond.

"She started a month ago," Danjiel said, flushing red under the hetman's gaze.

"What other symptoms does she have? Has the doctor seen her?"

"Oh, she has no symptoms. She just chooses not to speak," Danjeel said as Marjiana nodded.

Garuhj seemed unsure of himself. "I will ask the Fenon to come by."

Marjiana frowned and shook her head, with a finality anyone might have understood.

"Of course, I understand, but what about your sons?" the hetman stammered.

"It's no problem," Jeriem, her youngest, said. "We understand her fine."

Garuhj looked as though he wanted to say more, to argue that Jeriem could not possibly be telling the truth, but a look from Marjiana stopped him short. She led her sons back home, aware as she left the celebration that a number of those present had been watching her conversation with the hetman very closely.

Marjiana was out in the fields by first light after finishing her solitary coffee, checking each of the tender shoots that had sprouted this season for any sign of rot. One of the things they had come to realize, in the ten years since the first rot had appeared, was that any plants with the disease had to be removed immediately, or the disease would quickly spread to the others. It was painstaking work, but they did not have the machines to do it for them. They had lost so many people to the fevers they could only keep enough in working order to do the most labor intensive of tasks, such as harvesting or planting.

Her sons joined her, one by one, as they finished their breakfasts. Kjessel remained in the house, in bed. The melancholy that had seized him nearly three years ago had not relented its grip. Nor would it, Marjiana suspected. He was an engineer and used to problems having solutions, an inner logic. There had been little of that these last years.

In the two years since the celebration day for their arrival upon the terraformed planet, when it had become generally known that she no longer spoke, Marjiana had become a figure of intense fascination for those who remained from among the initial settlers. Some, like the hetman, unsure of her silence, suspected her of some ulterior motive, though they could not have said what. Others saw her as a religious figure of some vague sort, a bringer of salvation. There were even whispers that she had received a sign from God, though what god that could be, no one could say.

She was none of these things, she was just Marjiana, and she felt no need to explain herself, just as she no longer felt any particular need to speak. That part of her life was over and what little—for it seemed more and more

likely their lives here would not be lengthy ones—
remained to her would be spent as she chose it. The boys
had understood, or at least accepted it, adapting easily to
this new silent world. Kjessel was lost to her, as so many
had become lost over these last years.

Marjiana straightened up, flexing her left hip gingerly.
Her side ached when she walked or did any kind of
physical labor. It was a dull pain, one that she had grown
used to over the last weeks since her injury. There was
nothing else to do but become accustomed to it. Fenon,
the community doctor, had succumbed to the fevers last
year. Now they made do with what little those who were
left knew.

She caught sight of Danjesh making his way from his
own home to the fields and waved at him. He returned her
wave and called out, "How's things Marjiana?"

She gave a shrug and a twist of her one hand, a gesture
all the settlers used to indicate that all was well, more or
less.

Danjesh nodded. "Might rain. Best take care with your
walk."

Marjiana gestured that she would. In addition to her
silence, her daily walks beyond the settlement had become
common knowledge among the settlers. She had never
told anyone, not even her sons, where she went on these,
and this too had added to the fascination many had with
her. As well as deepening the mistrust of those who saw
the mystery of her silence as a threat. It would have been a
hard thing to explain to anyone, even if she were willing to,
but it was a thing she did for herself alone.

Danjesh walked on to the far fields he was responsible
for, past the five other homesteads that made up the outer
ring of the settlement. Beyond them the terraformed land
held sway. Two of the five houses were uninhabited, the
families there having passed from the fever along with the
doctor. Two others were not empty, but might as well
have been, for their inhabitants had fallen into despair and

now spent their days indoors awaiting their end. The hetman came once a week, trying to stir them from their melancholy, to no effect.

It was hard to blame them, in so many ways. There had been little of anything beyond mistakes and their ill consequences, these last years. They all lived with it, as best they could. Some better than others. Marjiana had learned to prepare for the worst. The universe was rarely kind and beneficent and one had to fight for the scraps of happiness that could be found, lest someone else steal them away.

"I don't understand. It should be working. There's no reason for it not to be." Kjessel frowned and attempted, for the fourth time, to restart the planter. They had been trying to get it to work for over an hour now.

Marjiana watched him patiently, not saying anything. It had been one thing after another these last years, after the initial excitement of their arrival in this newly formed world had given way to the tedium and desperation of living in it. More and more desperation seemed to be arriving everyday.

"It has to be in the circuits somehow, but I don't see anything wrong," Kjessel added, more to himself than to her.

The terraforming had been completed over three years while most of the settlers slept in cryofreeze, with only the captain and few others there to oversee the process. It was all computer models and programs anyway. The settlers, nearly ten thousand strong, had built an initial settlement in the temperate zone, where agriculture was expected to be good, with two crops being taken off the land in a good year.

The first two seasons were such a success—the seed banks the vessel carried all seeming to take to the new world's soil—that they had not even needed to utilize the five years of food supplies their vessel contained. Those were saved, in the event of a crop failure or other emergency in the years that followed. And those emergencies had arrived, one after the other.

"Why don't we leave it for now and have lunch," Marjiana said, when it became apparent that Kjessel's frustrations were becoming too great and no solution was at hand. "Take your mind from it and we'll come back to it later."

Kjessel relented, though he kept muttering to himself on the way back to their house. "I don't understand. I don't understand."

A group of one thousand had decided to begin a second settlement, about twenty kilometers away, in their third year. They were the ones who brought the first word of the rot in the plants that ate up entire crops. Much research was done, but no one could explain it, and the settlers moved back to the main settlement before the year was out. The next year the rot spread to the main settlement. And a group of explorers who had left in the first year, seeking to survey as much of the newly formed planet as possible, returned, half of their group having died of a mysterious fever.

Now this season, their equipment, expected to last them for ten years or more, had mysteriously begun to fail. Again, no explanation could be found, though Kjessel desperately sought one.

"I don't understand," he would say day after day, one failure after another.

This was not how it was supposed to be, was the subtext of what he was saying. The hardest years were supposed to be past them by now, the settlement established and the crops flourishing. That was true in successful colonies, of course. The history of the failed ones was grimmer, and largely unknown. For who was left to tell it, to warn others against their failures?

The sky was grey with cloud that promised rain, as

Danjesh had predicted. Marjiana eyed it with distrust as she set off down the road. She had learned to prepare for the worst. Danjesh's concern was warranted, for, in spite of the supposed temperate climate they had settled in, on those rare occasions when it did rain, it came in such endless torrents that rivers and lakes formed and could flood half the territory in a matter of minutes. The worst of all worlds.

With her bad hip, Marjiana would have little hope of getting to high ground before a flash flood consumed her. Yet that did not stop her from continuing on toward the last of the settlements, where the road ended and there was only the barest of trails, marked largely by her own footsteps. This was the part of the day, aside from her morning coffee, that she treasured the most. She would risk flood and death for this daily walk; the destination was worth it, and so little else was.

She walked past the final house at the settlement's edge, where the widow Annys lived, another of those who had succumbed to melancholy. It was almost as infectious as the fevers. And nearly as deadly, Marjiana thought, recalling those who had taken their lives rather than suffer any longer.

Kjessel had tried twice already, and one day, she knew, he would succeed. Marjiana, or one of their sons, would not be there to save him. In some ways, it would be a blessing. Not for their sons, who would desperately miss their father, but for Kjessel. And for her, if she could admit it. She hated to see the man she loved suffer so, and that suffering would not end, not in this place.

As she came abreast of Annys' house, the hetman ducked out of the door, adjusting his pants and his shirt, a satisfied smile on his face. It disappeared as he saw Marjiana and met her gaze, replaced by a watchful unease. He did not know how to act around her. Many did not.

"Well met, Sister Marjiana," Garuhj said, unable to disguise his discomfort. "Well met. The family is well? I was just calling on Sister Annys, to see that all is well with her."

Marjiana gave the same twist of her hand that she had earlier to Danjeesh. All was well. Garuhj frowned, clearly irritated by her silence.

"Still pretending at being a mute, I see," he said. "Don't think that I don't know what you're about."

It was Marjiana's turn to frown, but hers was out of confusion. She had no idea what the hetman might be talking about. Did he think her refusal to speak was part of some grand plan aimed at him? In response she gave a helpless shrug, to indicate she did not understand.

Garuhj glared at her. "Don't try this game with me? It may work on these other rubes, but not me. I was chosen hetman. You have to answer me."

Marjiana had to resist a smile. She stared at him, not speaking, her face without expression.

"What is your damn problem?" the hetman said, as she remained still, unwavering in her gaze. "I was providing comfort to a broken woman. I don't need to explain myself to the likes of you. At least I am doing what I can to save this community."

Marjiana shrugged and nodded. Garuhj did not need to justify himself to her. She did not care, as should have been plain by now. Stepping past him, she continued on to the end of the road and then beyond.

"I'm watching you sister," Garuhj called after her.

She offered no response, not even glancing back until she was well past the settlement, the houses specks upon the horizon. When she did, she saw that the hetmans was following behind her.

The silence was the first thing Marjiana became aware of as she drifted back into consciousness, slowly becoming alert to her surroundings. It took her several minutes to open her eyes and when she did, she found all she could see was a blur of colors. It was some time before they resolved themselves into coherent shapes.

She attempted to move and found she could not. Her body was leaden and unresponsive; she could not even turn her head. Not that she would have wanted to.

Before her was a viewfinder through which she could see the newly terraformed planet that awaited her and the rest of the settlers below. It was breathtaking to look at from so far above: the swirling white of the clouds crossing over the deep blue of the ocean and the green and brown of the landmasses.

As she stared at it in wonder, her emotions overwhelming her, only one thought occurred to her: this was home.

The impression, and the emotions that came with it, were fleeting. Her body gradually adjusted to being awake after so long in hibernation, the after-effects of the cryofreeze dimming slightly. She was able to move a little and became aware of what was happening around her. The soft murmur of conversations drifted by her ears, puncturing the cocoon she had lain in for those brief seconds.

I will remember this, she told herself, *I will remember this for the rest of my days.*

At first Marjiana just ignored the fact that Garuhj was following her, assuming he would realize the foolishness of what he was doing eventually and turn back. He did not though, and she was forced to stop and wait for him. She felt as irritated as he had been at her, and no doubt still was.

Why did he care that she chose not to speak? She paid no mind to what he did and gave no thought to what he was doing with the widow Annys. It did not matter to her. There were troubles enough in this world, she did not need to find others.

When the hetman caught up with her he was belligerent and sneering. "Ready to talk now, are you?"

Marjiana shook her head.

"Look, you and I need to come to an understanding. I am the hetman of this place. I can't be keeping order and dealing with some sort of religious nonsense, or whatever this is. People need hope, not delusion."

Marjiana kept staring at Garuhj, her expression firm and unchanging.

The hetman's fury seemed to blossom in the face of her silence. "I will not let some mad woman bring me down. I am the only thing keeping this community together. You may have given up on life, but I haven't. I won't. I will do whatever needs doing to keep this community alive and hopeful."

The last sounded like a threat, which made Marjiana raise an eyebrow. She set her jaw and braced herself for whatever the hetman had planned. How to explain to him that she had not given up on life, or their community, they just defined hope in different ways. Even if she were willing to give voice to this thought, she knew her words would not reach him.

"Do not force me to act," Garuhj said. "I will do what I must to protect the community. I am the hetman. I will not be intimidated by the likes of you."

Marjiana stood her ground, not altering her expression in the least. The hetman took a step forward, a menacing sneer curling his lips. When she did not react he took another step forward, leaning down so that his face was right before hers. Marjiana did not break her gaze from his eyes, though she could feel his breath on her cheeks.

Seconds passed with neither of them moving, the tension palpable. Marjiana had a strange urge to laugh, her lips twitching into a smile she had to fight to control. Garuhj wet his lips and flared his nostrils, but otherwise did not move. She wondered how long they would stand there, and what she would do if the hetman actually carried through with his threat.

Marjiana never had to answer those questions.

Something shifted in Garuhj's expression and he could no longer meet her eyes. He turned around, without a word, and walked back toward the settlement. Marjiana watched him for a time, to assure herself that he was truly leaving her be, before turning and resuming her walk.

The journey took her close to an hour, through the rolling hills of the plain they had established their settlement on. There were few trees in this region of the planet, giving her an incredible view of the vast sky above stretching on into an apparently endless horizon. The limitlessness of the horizon always calmed her, which she needed today after her confrontation with the hetman. That battle was not over yet, she knew, and that worried her a little. A problem for another day.

When she had first begun her walks they had been aimless, just an excuse for her to get away and be by herself. After so many years in the midst of their tiny, and ever-shrinking community, she felt she deserved some time to herself. She had explored the surrounding area, until she came across the place she was going to now. Once she found it her walks had changed. They had only one destination.

It was a natural spring, hidden in amongst a circle of hills. A few short trees with long, wispy leaves, that made the branches appear to be weeping, grew around it. The hills protected the spring from the wind, making the water and the trees still, and giving the place a feeling of a world apart.

The world around her was quiet, not a sound from the settlement reaching her, not even a whisper of a breeze. Marjiana sat, as she always did, at the spring's edge, staring down at the water. The sky, in all its glorious blue and drifting white clouds, was reflected in the still pool, and she watched it with rapt attention. And she remembered.

IF YOU ENJOYED
THE FARTHEST REACHES,
YOU MIGHT ALSO LIKE:

THE FORGOTTEN
VOLUME ONE OF THE SOJOURNERS
CYCLE

Who is David Aeida? And what does he know that has so many people pursuing him?

David doesn't know. He can't remember anything about who he is. But he finds himself ensnared in a vicious conflict between a religious cult and a guild that patrols the crossings between multiple universes. They will both stop at nothing to gain whatever knowledge he possesses. Most dangerous of all, is the implacable hunter, known only as the Seeker, who has his own reasons for wanting to find David.

His only hope is to recover his memories before they do. His only ally is a woman named Meredith, and she definitely knows more than she is telling...

1

I remember nothing but this moment right now, as I walk through this park alone. Before, there was only darkness—not even darkness, something without substance at all. I emerged, whole but flailing, my feet carrying me forward before any thought or awareness had taken form. It is as though all that had been left behind, scraped away, in my journey from the void to this place.

The park is the sort one can find in any city, with grass and trees, footpaths winding their way through the greenery, and benches set at intervals upon which people sit. The surrounding neighborhood is equally unremarkable, a mixture of houses and apartment buildings with not a landmark among them. There is what looks like a school at the park's far end, with a yard fenced off from the rest of the park and turned into soccer and baseball fields.

I have no memories. How did I come to be here? Clearly I was walking from somewhere, with some destination in mind. These facts elude me.

My perception seems heightened, my senses keen to the slightest shifts in shadow and light, a breeze the cause of astonishment. It is as though I have been denied these basic sensations for so long that a minuscule change appears momentous. A cacophony of sound reaches my ears: the symphony of leaves rustling, the hum of cars on pavement, and the indecipherable murmurs of people around me. As they pass by I am entranced by their expressions, fleeting emotions slipping across their face that it seems only I am aware of.

Ahead of me a dog barks, quick and sharp, cutting through the clatter of sound and drawing my focus. It is led by a couple, perhaps in their early fifties. I follow them as they go along the path, listening to their conversation, though it is in a language I do not recognize. He appears to be Japanese, though I am certain that is not the language he is speaking. This seems significant to me and I listen to each intonation the couple makes, certain somehow that if I can unravel this code I can understand what is happening.

No meaning comes to me, and when they turn to the left to continue on the path around the park, I keep going straight, heading down the nearest street. At the next corner I turn right, my legs seeming to remember what my mind cannot. I trust them, going where instinct leads me, trying to empty my mind of any thought. Eventually I come to an apartment building, five or six stories tall, white and sickly green colors marking its exterior. I stand uneasily by the door until I fish in my jacket pocket and find a set of keys, one of which works, so I let myself in.

The air in the lobby is very warm, as if someone had left the heat on, even though it feels like summer. There is an odd, malingering odor; old carpets and humidity, I think. The lobby is filled with fake plants and battered furniture, remnants of a previous age. There is a mailroom to my left and a man steps out from it, a clutch of fliers in his hand, startling me. He seems not to notice my surprise, giving me the briefest of glances and a nod. Has he recognized me, or is he simply being polite?

I follow him upstairs, automatically continuing on to

the third floor as he steps off at the second, and find myself before room 304. I try my keys, knocking on the door as I unlock it, and enter.

"Hello," I call out tentatively, the sound of my voice shocking me.

I ignore that for the moment, ignore the creeping sense of terror I feel at all the blank spaces around my thoughts. Instead I explore the apartment, trying desperately to find something I recognize and can cling to in this storm of the unfamiliar. I go from the kitchen to the living room to the bedroom, opening closets and drawers. There are several bookshelves and I study their contents, as well as the CDs and movies spread out on the floor by the television and stereo. None of it stirs anything in me.

As I feel panic begin to seize me, my throat constricting and my hands going numb, a thought occurs to me and I go into the bathroom. I stand in the darkness for a moment, gathering myself, before flicking on the light. At the sight of those blinking eyes, that open mouth, those lips and that hair, I fall to the floor. I am numb everywhere, the blood seeming to leave my body. I clench my arms around my chest and shiver.

There is a voice repeating something over and over. At first it startles me, and I wonder if someone has followed me, or if I turned on the television somehow, but then I realize it is my voice, that my mouth is moving, my tongue and lips forming these words. It does not seem possible. None of this is possible. I know nothing of myself, not my name, who I was, or what I am doing here, but I know, with a certainty so absolute it terrifies me, that the person returning my gaze in the mirror is not me.

2

I crawl from the bathroom, choking back sobs, my whole body shaking with fear and revulsion. I want to peel off this skin, cut off my nose and lips, all of my face. Perhaps beneath it all is the person I am, not this simulacrum. But who is that exactly? I have no sense, no idea of where to even begin. My mind is blank, my thoughts as unfamiliar as the face that stares back at me, though they tantalize at moments, almost seeming to be my own. My instincts have returned me to this place, it is all here somewhere within me. But for now I remain a foreign country to myself.

When I have recovered from my shock enough to get to my feet, I go to the kitchen to see if there is anything to drink. I fumble through the cupboards haphazardly, my search of the apartment only moments before already forgotten, and come across a bottle of rye and some packets of chai tea. I opt for the tea, not trusting my stomach with the alcohol, though the thought of oblivion is tempting. I find the kettle and fill it with water and plug it in, spending a few anxious moments waiting for it to come to a boil.

A phone begins to ring as I wait for the tea to finish steeping. I locate it in the bedroom atop a dresser amidst a scattering of detritus: loose change, receipts, and sunglasses, all stray pieces of a lost life. Looking at the display I see a name and a number and, while I try to call forth from my memory any details about the Meredith whose name appears there, the call goes to voicemail. The name does not seem familiar to me, but the number is a local one. How I know that I cannot say, but a quick search of the cell for its number shows the same area code. It seems likely that my instincts are correct again.

I nod to myself and go to have my tea, taking the phone with me. Opening up the missed call on the display, I find Meredith's contact and see that the only information I have on her is this phone number. Flipping through the log it appears that she called quite often, every two or three days in most cases. Strangely, or so I think, there are no outgoing calls from this phone to her and no texts in either direction. She is always calling here and the conversations were short, no more than ten minutes. Unusual for a friendship, so an acquaintance, then. But what sort?

Do I dare phone her back in my current state? I need answers, but it is impossible to say whether or not she has any, or whether I can trust her. The fact that there are no outgoing calls or texts to her number seems significant to me. As I mull these questions the phone starts to ring, vibrating insistently on the table. Meredith again. I stare at the display, a hundred competing thoughts racing through my mind, all ending with the face that stared back at me in the mirror and the depthless black that followed.

"Hello," I say, my hands shaking as I hold the phone to my ear.

"Where the hell have you been, David?" says the voice on the other end, without preamble.

"I was out for a walk," I say, after I have recovered from my surprise. My voice, strained and high, filled with tension and adrenaline, sounds more alien than ever to my ears. No more than the name she has just uttered, though, which I immediately feel cannot be mine.

"What a load of…" Her voice trails off in disgust. "Whatever. Look, we need to meet now, as soon as you can."

I hesitate, unsure what to make of her request. Whether due to her manner, or the clear anxiety that underlay it, I do not trust her. But her familiarity, her presumption to ask for a rendezvous, suggests we have done so before. Will refusing strike her as out of character? Will she insist on meeting, or worse, come over to the apartment? I do not want to face her now, not when I am still out of sorts, without any bearings. If I can delay her somehow…She does not give me the chance.

"I don't care if you don't want to," she says, cutting into my silence and reading my thoughts. "We have to meet and we can't afford to wait. They're coming for us. Do you understand? They've found us and they're here."

"Who?" I says, the question sounding stupid, even to my ears.

"What is the matter with you? I'm not talking about this over the phone, for God's sake."

"Sorry, Meredith. You just caught me at a bad time. I'm a little distracted is all."

There is a pause and I can hear her swear under her breath. "Forget about her. We've got bigger problems now. Do you know the Beano?"

"Sure," I say without hesitation, and am startled to realize that I do know exactly the place she is referring to.

"Good. I can be there in ten minutes. You better be there too."

She hangs up before I can say anything further. I hold the phone at my ear, listening to the vacuum on the other end, in a complete daze. At last I set it down and with an unsteady hand take a sip of my now lukewarm tea. *David*. It just doesn't sound right. Nothing felt right about me; it is like an itch I cannot scratch.

There is something not right about Meredith too, I can feel it through the phone. I don't trust her. The threat she mentioned, is that real? It's impossible for me to judge. What seems certain is that she knew plenty about me—the woman she mentioned, for one—and she might very well be able to help with all the questions I have. But do I want to hear the answers?

3

The Cafe Beano is a coffee shop on the corner of a busy avenue not far from the apartment building, a place I am convinced I have been before, though no memory comes to me. Yet I know where it is and can picture its cluttered interior, with tables and chairs strewn about seemingly at random, can smell the bitter coffee and hear the chatter of the menagerie of people gathered within its walls.

It is the specificity of these memories that seems the strangest of all to me. Why can I recall with exacting detail everything about the Beano, but not remember having been there or anywhere else in this city, wherever it is? It's as if someone planted the memory whole within me, but left aside all the context, all the things that make a memory personal. This recollection could be anyone's, just as I could be anyone, and that is what bothers me most of all.

Meredith might be able to help there, I reason, as I walk back through the park to the coffee shop. All those things that seemed so significant earlier—the couple talking, the movement of the light through the tree branches, the damp smell of the earth—I note now in a glancing way, giving them no real thought, my mind on how to proceed with Meredith. Did I reveal to her that I have no memory of who I am? Can I trust her with this information? Best to wait until I better understand what she wants and go from there, I decide.

I have a sudden moment of panic as I step into the Cafe Beano, glancing about at the faces of those sitting at the tables or standing in line for coffee, and realize I have no idea what Meredith looks like. If she is already here I have no way of finding her—how did this not occur to me before, I wonder, feeling my face go red—and there will be no hiding my memory loss from her. Realizing there is nothing else for it now that I am here, I go and stand in line, fidgeting and glancing about to see if anyone in the place is trying to meet my eyes.

As I wait, a slim woman, with hair that wavered between blond and brown, depending on the light, pulled tight into a dancer's bun that peaked atop her head, comes alongside me and says in a quiet voice, so unlike the one she used on the phone, "I'll get a table at the back. Get me a latte."

I nod, our eyes meeting and lingering, before she slips by, disappearing behind me. That brief moment of contact, electric with unspoken thoughts and emotions I cannot even begin to parse, unsettles me deeply. The low level of anxiety I have felt from the moment I stepped into the cafe, overfull with people, talk, and heat, blossoms within me now that this confrontation is at hand.

It is all too much, too quickly. I still haven't recovered from my first glimpse of myself, still do not feel comfortable, even to stand in line, my body, too large or small or just wrong. And now I am out under the unforgiving gaze of others, who I imagine can somehow pierce through whatever disguise I have on and see the falseness at my core.

The woman behind the counter smiles at me as my turn comes to order. "Back already," she says and, when I look at her blankly, adds, "You were just here this morning."

"Right," I say, nodding, not saying anything else and looking away.

The next thing I know I am walking away, coffee in hand. I do not remember ordering or paying, though I must have. My breathing is unsteady and sounds loud in my ears and my hands are numb, so that with each step I worry I will drop the cups. Stopping to gather myself, I see Meredith watching me from a table by the window at the back of the cafe, her face unreadable. The table is near a door leading out to a patio where a few smokers linger, and I note that she will have a clear view of both entrances, as well as the whole of the place. That is not an accident, I think, as I start toward her.

"What is the matter with you?" she says as I sit down. "I thought you were going to faint right there."

I shrug, passing her the latte, and took the lid off mine to blow on it. "Just had a moment."

"What does that mean?" she says, and then waves a hand in exasperation. "Never mind. We've got more important things to talk about."

"You said they were here looking for us?"

Meredith leans forward, her eyes darting around, pitching her voice low. "You remember what I told you about them?"

"Who?" I say automatically, forgetting myself. I flush red, almost wincing as Meredith's steady eyes try to read mine.

"I'm not going to say their name," she says, as though I could not be a greater fool. "You know who. They've brought a Seeker over here."

"Over here?" I say. Something about the way she emphasizes those words draws my attention.

"Here," she says. "If they have a Seeker they will find us. It's a matter of time."

I nod as though I understand. Meredith looks doubtful and she seems about to say something else when her gaze is drawn to the cafe's main entrance. Seeing her eyes transfixed, horror and fear growing in them, I turn to look and see two men standing in the doorway casting their hard eyes around the room as if they are looking for someone.

They are massive in size, tall and broad-shouldered, their muscle evident even beneath the long jackets they wear. Except they are not jackets I notice, as I look closer, more like robes, black in color, except for the red symbol upon the shoulder. Something tugs at my mind as I stare at them, trying to remember where I have seen the figure before, a thought almost taking shape.

It does not come, for the two men step aside and a third comes into view. He is much shorter than they, with a slight build, wearing a similar cut robe, though his is dark grey. His head is almost entirely covered by a grey scarf, the wrapping not unlike that for a turban, leaving only his eyes visible, and those only after a fashion, for he is wearing what appears to be a mutant pair of aviator goggles. The lenses are a deep violet the light reflects strangely off of. It seems impossible that their wearer could see anything out of them. There are no straps extending from the goggles and, as I look closer to determine how they are kept in place, I realize they are fused to his skin in some manner.

As I am wondering how that can be possible, Meredith is standing and taking me by the arm.

"Don't look at them," she whispers, as she pulls me from my chair toward the door. "We have to go."

Dumbfounded by everything that is happening, I let her lead me out the door, though my body feels limp and it is a struggle to move.

"Quickly," Meredith says, her hand pressing hard on my arm as she leads me down the street. "Don't look back."

I am unable to stop myself, though; I have to see the man with the impossible eyes and the robes with the rune I can almost recall having seen before. As I turn to get my last glimpse, Meredith jerking my shoulder hard and swearing at me under her breath, I can just see three of them. They have moved to the center of the cafe, their presence drawing curious stares from those sitting nearby. The man with the grotesque eyes is staring out the window in our direction. I feel a chill run up my spine as I can feel his alien gaze fall upon me.

"They see us," I say to Meredith.

"We'll have to run."

THE FORGOTTEN is now available.

ABOUT THE AUTHOR

Clint Westgard is the author of The Shadow Men Trilogy and the science fiction epic The Sojourners Cycle. In addition, he has published a work of historical fantasy set in colonial Peru, The Maleficio Chronicles, and a retelling of the Minotaur legend, The Trials of the Minotaur. Clint Westgard lives in Calgary, Alberta.

ALSO BY CLINT WESTGARD

The Forgotten
Volume One of The Sojourners Cycle

Who is David Aeida? And what does he know that has so
many people pursuing him?

David doesn't know. He can't remember anything about
who he is. But he finds himself ensnared in a vicious
conflict between a religious cult and a guild that patrols the
crossings between multiple universes. They will both stop
at nothing to gain whatever knowledge he possesses. Most
dangerous of all, is the implacable hunter, known only as
the Seeker, who has his own reasons for wanting to find
David.

His only hope is to recover his memories before they do.
His only ally is a woman named Meredith, and she
definitely knows more than she is telling...

Spanning both universes and the human mind, The
Forgotten is an unforgettable science fiction thriller that
questions the very nature of identity. It is the first volume
of the Sojourners Cycle, an epic that will encompass the
fates of universes and humanity itself.

ALSO BY CLINT WESTGARD

The Apostate
Volume Two of The Sojourners Cycle

Laila has only one goal in mind. To have her revenge upon the Grand Regent for all he has done to her. First, though, she needs to find her way across the universes.

That is easier said than done. The Grand Regent's agents are still pursuing her. As is the Society of Travellers. And the Seeker lurks somewhere, waiting for his moment to strike.

Laila has a plan, though, and a few tricks of her own. But she will discover that not everything is at seems. For the war she has given her life to hides a far greater conflict.

Spanning multiple universes and the complexities of the human mind, The Apostate, continues the incredible journey begun in The Forgotten. The second volume of The Sojourners Cycle is an unforgettable science fiction epic that encompasses the fates of universes and humanity itself.

ALSO BY CLINT WESTGARD

The Acolyte
Volume Three of The Sojourners Cycle

After crossing the universes to join with Toma Osahi's group of renegades in their battle for control of the Church of Regents, Laila finds herself in a precarious position. While they both share the same goal—the destruction of the Grand Regent—Osahi doesn't know who Laila really is. What will he do if he finds out?

While Laila struggles to keep her identity secret, Osahi and his people pull her deeper and deeper into a search for Ana that promises to shed light on the dark secrets of the Watchers' Order and the Acolytes. Before she can find those answers though, Laila will have to face what lies within.

Crossing the universes has unsettled the already shaky equilibrium in her mind. If she wants to return herself to her own body, she will have to act fast, for the consequences of what Acolytes did to her are still reverberating. And Aeida hides somewhere, waiting for his time to come.

The thrilling third volume of the Sojourners Cycle continues Laila's incredible journey across the universes against incredible odds, as well as exploring her past, including the pivotal role she played in the rise of the Grand Regent and her own downfall at his hands.

ALSO BY CLINT WESTGARD

The Double
Volume Four of The Sojourners Cycle

David Aeida now commands his body, having cast Laila
aside. He has sworn fealty to the Grand Regent, who
wants him by his side and sees that his loyalty is rewarded.

But the Grand Regent is not the man he was. He is
paranoid and suspicious of everyone, isolated in his tower,
and thirsting for vengeance against those he feels have
wronged him. How long until he turns on Aeida as well?

That is only the beginning of Aeida's problems. For he
knows the Seeker and the Society of Travelers remain to
play their parts. Both desire nothing more than the utter
destruction of the Church of Regents and all its works.
And though Laila has been defeated, he knows better than
anyone not to assume she has been vanquished.

The epic fourth volume of the Sojourners Cycle centers
upon the many betrayals and lies at the heart of the faith of
the Church of Regents and the devastation upon the lives
of the faithful they have wrought. Desire and guilt, love
and revenge, rage and despair will drive them all, with
consequences for all the universes.

ALSO BY CLINT WESTGARD

The Sojourner
Volume Five of The Sojourners Cycle

Laila's strange and reluctant alliance with the Seeker continues, though she does not know where it will lead her. She fears it will place her in another prison, worse than the one she has just managed to escape.

But her escape is not entirely complete. For though she has been restored to her own flesh, parts of Aeida somehow still remain. Along with some other she does not recognize. Is this some aftereffect of the Acolyte's bizarre procedure? Or the result of the Seeker's meddling?

All this pales in comparison to what Laila soon discovers. That she has an unwanted part to play in an ancient struggle for who will rule the crossings between the universes and all that lies in them.

In the stunning conclusion to the Sojourners Cycle Laila will be faced with a terrible choice, one that will decide her fate and humanity's.

ALSO BY CLINT WESTGARD

Realm of Shadows
Volume One of The Shadow Men

Craitol and Renuih, two empires a world apart, divided by the desert that lies between them. A desert ruled by the Shadow Men.

An uneasy peace holds sway in both realms, hiding longstanding feuds and bitter rivalries. Until a Shadow Men raid on Renuih shatters the calm and sets in motion events no one can control.

Masiph id Ezern, unfavored son of the Imperial Vazeir, finds himself a hero following the raid. His father remains unmoved by his exploits and, in his bitterness, Masiph will find himself a reluctant participant in a plot against the empire.

As he finds himself drawn deeper and deeper into the conspiracy, he soon realizes there will be no escaping the realm of shadows, where intrigue and betrayal abound. And though the Shadow Men have gone quiet, they will not stay silent forever...

ALSO BY CLINT WESTGARD

Council of Shadows
Volume Two of The Shadow Men

Discontent continues to fester within the realms of Craitol and Renuih, fed by intrigues carried out in the shadows. As rivals and apostates struggle for supremacy, a long incubated plan begins to unfold.

Vyissan, a mysterious alkemycal practitioner arrives in Renuih, the latest strike in a long war over who shall control the secrets of alkemya and Craitol itself. He carries with him a secret that, once revealed, will reverberate across all realms. Before he can reveal it though, the conspirators against the emperor will strike their own blow.

But now, a new and more powerful menace looms on the horizon. The Shadow Men have gained the secrets of the Council Adept's alkemya and no one can be certain what they will do with it…

ALSO BY CLINT WESTGARD

Dance of Shadows
Volume Three of The Shadow Men

War with the Shadow Men looms in both realms as the consequences of the Gvers' Council in Craitol begin to make themselves known. A war that could end in glorious triumph or bitter disaster.

Doubt shadows everyone's steps, for they know there are no certainties in the desert. Especially now the Shadow Men have made the art of alkemya their own.

No one has more questions than Vyissan, for he is working in service to a cause he is no longer sure he believes in. And now he must undertake a journey with those who both loathe and fear him. Before the first sword is drawn, his life will be under threat.

But his will not be the only one, for somewhere in the desert the Shadow Men lie in wait…

ALSO BY CLINT WESTGARD

The Maleficio Chronicles

Luisa is always more than she appears. Rumor and mystery surround her. And strange events seem to follow wherever she goes.

Born in Lima, City of Kings, to a noble family, her father so fears her true nature that he banishes her to a convent. There she falls under the suspicion of the Inquisition and decides to flee.

Disguised as a man, she embarks upon a series of wild adventures, dueling, carousing, and gambling her way across colonial Peru. But everything changes when someone recognizes her for what she truly is, and soon she finds herself fighting for her very survival.

In a world where she will always stand apart, Luisa undergoes a strange journey, marked by betrayal and murder, terrible powers and mysterious strangers. *The Maleficio Chronicles* is her incredible confession and a story like no other.

ALSO BY CLINT WESTGARD

The Devious Kind

A Mystery

The body of a local woman is found in a coulee on a ranch north of Loverna, her head blown off with a shotgun. New to town and the job, Constable Martin Thomas arrives on the scene as a spring snowstorm begins to wipe out all evidence before his investigation has even begun.

There is no shortage of suspects to consider. A spurned husband. A jealous lover. A betrayed business partner. And family members battling over an inheritance. All have motive and opportunity. And no one seems to be telling him everything.

As he tries to sift the truth from the lies, the snowstorm continues to build, leaving Loverna cut off from the outside world. And Thomas alone to face a killer who will do anything not to get caught.